THE ANIMALS

THE
ANIMALS

Cary Fagan

BOOK*HUG PRESS
Toronto 2022

FIRST EDITION

Library and Archives Canada Cataloguing in Publication

Title: The animals / Cary Fagan.
Names: Fagan, Cary, author.
Identifiers: Canadiana (print) 20220217092 | Canadiana (ebook) 20220217106
   ISBN 9781771667647 (softcover)
   ISBN 9781771667654 (EPUB)
   ISBN 9781771667661 (PDF)
Classification: LCC PS8561.A375 A79 2022 | DDC C813/.54—dc23

The production of this book was made possible through the generous assistance of the Canada Council for the Arts and the Ontario Arts Council. Book*hug Press also acknowledges the support of the Government of Canada through the Canada Book Fund and the Government of Ontario through the Ontario Book Publishing Tax Credit and the Ontario Book Fund.

 Canada Council for the Arts   Conseil des Arts du Canada   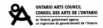 ONTARIO ARTS COUNCIL CONSEIL DES ARTS DE L'ONTARIO an Ontario government agency un organisme du gouvernement de l'Ontario

 Canada    ONTARIO CREATES | ONTARIO CRÉATIF

Book*hug Press acknowledges that the land on which we operate is the traditional territory of many nations, including the Mississaugas of the Credit, the Anishnabeg, the Chippewa, the Haudenosaunee, and the Wendat peoples. We recognize the enduring presence of many diverse First Nations, Inuit, and Métis peoples and are grateful for the opportunity to meet and work on this territory.

To Frank W. Watt
for his encouragement all those years ago

❧ 1 ❧

Secrets

Dorn, whose profession was the making of miniature scale models, was not usually embarrassed by his commissions. It might be said that he was locally famous; even if people in the village didn't know his name, they were familiar with his models, which were displayed in the windows of almost every shop, restaurant, and business. There were also half a dozen in the municipal museum, all from businesses that had closed. While Dorn often worried that he would run out of commissions, there seemed to be just enough shop turnover to keep him occupied.

This new project was for yet another new enterprise beside the hardware store. For some reason, nothing seemed to survive in that location for long; Dorn had completed commissions for a wool shop, a vacuum cleaner store, and a wedding gift emporium, the models all now in the museum. The new one, called the Velvet Touch, was a sex shop. It carried all sorts of creams and sprays, battery-operated devices, visual materials, and manuals, as well as costumes made of spandex and artificial leather and chains. It seemed to Dorn rather doubtful that the Velvet Touch was going to prosper when the other shops hadn't, especially since customers could easily be spied ducking inside from the main street.

Stooped over his bench in the ground-floor workshop at the back of his small house, Dorn worked on the scene. A tiny male figure, his even tinier penis erect, was tied to a bed while a woman in a peek-a-boo bra leaned over him with a whip. To better visualize the scale, one might imagine the whip as being the length of a toothpick. The model was near to being finished; at this moment, Dorn was using his finest brush to add shading to the man's penis and then to the woman's nipples.

Everyone has secrets—countless secrets that are neither important nor particularly interesting. Only a very few have secrets of any consequence, and Dorn was not one of them. These dull truths get added to as one gets older, and a new, ridiculous one for Dorn was that every time he worked on his miniature woman, which could have fit into the palm of a large hand, he felt the stirrings of an erection. Now was no exception. He felt only a mild shame, however; the arousal was understandable given the celibate life he had been leading since his last girlfriend had left three years before. The woman hadn't been from the village but rather the city. Like so many outsiders, she had come on a holiday, only to "fall in love" with the charms of the place. Dorn had wondered whether she was confusing her infatuation for the village with her feelings for him. But he had put these doubts aside and tried to be happy. Unfortunately, his first thought had been the correct one, and as her enthusiasm for village life withered, so had her affection for Dorn.

Now Dorn straightened up, feeling an ache between his shoulder blades. He was thirty-eight years old and already experiencing some of the pangs of oncoming middle age. He went to the washroom sink and cleaned the brushes and palette, scrubbed his hands, and hung his canvas smock on a hook. From the cupboard behind the small oval mirror, he took two brushes: one for his fair hair, which he kept long enough to fall over his eyes if he didn't brush it away, and one for the short, reddish beard that adorned his narrow face. He had no illusions about being handsome—his eyes were a little droopy and his nose was crooked—but he liked to appear neat (a habit, no doubt, that came naturally to a maker of miniatures), and after this grooming he took the few steps needed to reach his front hall, put on a cotton jacket, slipped off his work sandals and slipped on his outdoor sandals, picked up his battered paperback copy of *Vordram*, and left the house.

2

Happy Café

Dorn lived on Linder Row, which ran above and parallel to the main street. He walked down, passing the various restaurants and shops, each with one of his miniature scenes in the window. Preferring not to see his own work, he was careful to keep his gaze turned to the street.

The Happy Café, almost exactly in the centre of the shopping row, was not at all like sophisticated city coffee houses, with their reclaimed wood tables and local art on the walls, or their clean modernist lines. Instead, it had an ornate gable over the door and wood trim inside that made it look like a storybook cottage. The staff wore little suede dresses or shorts with suspenders and pointed hats with elfin ears. It had opened almost twenty years ago, when the village was trying to reinvent itself as a tourist attraction. The stone quarries to the south had become exhausted not long before, and a scheme to allow a multinational company to harvest the northern forest was halted by a legislative order. What if people, especially families, stayed three or four days, spending their money on restaurants, bed and breakfasts, attractions, souvenirs? The village council received grants to help transform businesses so that they looked like cabins, castles, or any sort of enchanted place, and the founders of the Happy Café took full advantage. So did Dorn's first customers, who wanted adorable window displays that might draw people inside.

The effort succeeded, although the initial surge of interest in earlier years had naturally slowed until now the village catered to a modest trade. There was even a challenger to the Happy Café in the form of a modern coffee chain at the far end of the main street. Dorn, however, remained a loyal customer. The reason was simple: Ravenna.

Ravenna was a loyal customer, too.

He entered the café, pushing through the curtain of beads. It was a little warm and humid, pleasantly womb-like, a place where one might curl up and fall into the deepest sleep. But his senses woke on seeing Ravenna, who had the corner table and sat with a cup and her usual folder of student work, which she seemed to be endlessly marking.

"Hey there, the usual double espresso?" said the elfin server behind the counter.

"Yes, Glin, thanks."

At the sound of his voice, Ravenna looked up and smiled, pushing away a few strands of hair that had escaped from her ponytail. Once she had been the villagers' hope for an athlete who could make the country's Olympics team. The village had belonged to one country and then another, and even a third for a short interval, and perhaps it was this historic identity crisis that made the prospect seem so exciting. Ravenna's sport had been the javelin throw, in which she had won local, regional, and then national competitions. Four years older than Ravenna, Dorn had seen her throw only once, when he was walking by the school's athletic field. Tall and willowy and a little awkward, she had reminded him of a giraffe. He had stood watching, entranced by her odd stance, her ungainly run, and then the force with which her slender arm hurled the javelin into the sky.

But Ravenna hadn't made the Olympics. She had decided not to try out for the national team but instead to immediately enter teachers college. There had even been a front page newspaper editorial begging her to reconsider. But that had been years ago and, so Ravenna claimed, meant nothing to the students in her classes now.

Dorn took his coffee and sat across from her. She made one more pencil mark and looked up at him. "Look at this student's work," she said. "It's a holy mess! How can anyone think clearly who's scribbling like this? It's hardly surprising that half the answers are wrong."

Dorn smiled, for he had noted that Ravenna had crumbs on her blouse, the remains of her dinklberry muffin. True, she wrote with extreme neatness, but everything else about her was charmingly dishevelled.

"My homework was always praised for neatness," Dorn said. "And I still received a bad grade in math. So I'm not sure what that proves."

"It proves that you didn't have a good teacher. You should have had me."

"No doubt. If I could have heard you above all the noise."

She gave him a look. "Where did you hear that?"

"A little bird told me."

In fact, it was Tul and Tule, the owners of the sex shop, whose nephew had reported that Ravenna's class was "super fun" because the teacher could hardly control her students.

"Anyway," she said, "a little anarchy can be good for the thinking process. And with all the other teachers so strict—"

"I assure you," Dorn interrupted her, "that I would have much preferred the atmosphere in your class."

"Okay, let's drop it. Are you doing anything tonight? I've got the Supper Club. We're going to that new bistro on Styvvin Place, it's supposed to be really good. They give us a special price in the hope that we'll tell our friends. There's always room for one more, if you want to come."

"You know I don't have gourmet tastes. I'm just as happy with a sausage and a beer. Your Supper Club friends would consider me a boor."

"And you're a reverse snob! You'd look down on them for caring about what they eat."

"That's true," Dorn said with a slightly forced chuckle.

"So you look down on *me*."

"I always look up to you, Ravenna. You're five centimetres taller than me."

"Ha ha, as if I haven't heard that joke a million times. Holy smokes, are you still reading *Vordram*? Thank God I don't teach the upper forms. See, I'm starting to yawn just thinking about that medieval tombstone. Isn't it like three hundred pages?"

"Just about. But it's different if you're reading it just for yourself. I missed it in school, during those months when I was home sick."

"Right, your mysterious illness. A severe allergy to school, probably."

"Maybe. That's when I started woodcarving. My uncle took pity on me being stuck at home and gave me an inexpensive set of tools."

"So something good came out of it. That doesn't mean you have to punish yourself by reading it now."

"It's different when it's a choice. I admit it's heavy going and I only get through a few pages at a time. But the poetic style is interesting, thirteen-syllable lines and with that scheme of stresses and internal rhyme—"

"Please!"

"Also, I think it really illuminates the national character."

"Well, listen to you. Maybe *you* should be the teacher."

"Right now I'm in the section where the Woodcutter, half starved, finds an unusual fruit growing from a tree in the forest. Do you remember it?"

"I remember only the agony of extreme boredom."

"He eats this fruit," Dorn went on, "and then lies down under the tree and has the strangest dream I've ever read in a book. He dreams that he sprouts breasts—large female breasts—on his arms and legs. And then, while he's staring at these protrusions—"

"Protrusions!"

"—a dozen infants suddenly appear. Infants with wings, flying down from the trees. Not angel-like at all. Scary. And each one attaches itself to a teat and begins sucking voraciously. The Woodcutter is naturally appalled—"

"Of course! He's appalled by a normal maternal act. Very much in keeping with your so-called national character. So what happens?"

"Never mind. Let's talk about something else."

"Come on, Dorn! I want to know. A teacher's education is never finished. What does the Woodcutter do?"

Dorn made a face and looked away. "He takes his axe."

"Oh, please! He kills the infants?"

"Not exactly. He cuts off each of his breasts."

"Oh, that's even more sick. Thanks for sharing, Dorn. And now my free period is almost over. I've got to rush back to school. Well, this has been most enlightening, Professor Dorn. Ta-ta!"

And with that, Ravenna shoved her folder into her bag, pulled her long legs from under the table, and hurried out of the café with a jokey wave. Dorn opened his book and read slowly, using the little spoon to scoop up the remaining coffee-soaked sugar granules at the bottom. After some time he got up, pushed in his chair, and put both his cup and Ravenna's (she always forgot) into the bin at the end of the counter.

"Can you do me a favour, Dorn?" called Glin, steaming milk for a new customer.

"What's that?"

"You're neighbours with Leev, aren't you?"

"That's right."

"He's ordered his usual bag of coffee beans. But he phoned to say that he can't come in to pick it up. Nobody's had a chance to run over there yet—do you think you might drop it off?"

"My pleasure."

"Fantastic. It's sitting beside the artificial-sugar packets. So what model are you working on now, Dorn? Anything interesting?"

"No," he replied quickly, picking up the bag of coffee beans. "Nothing very interesting." And then he went out again.

3

First Animal

Dorn walked one block south and turned off the main street. At that corner he passed Sizzel's Bookshop, the only long-established business that did not have one of his miniature models on display. In fact, old man Sizzel denounced all of the village's attempts to "sell this bullshit nostalgia," and Dorn couldn't help admiring him for it. There was nothing at all quaint about his bookshop, which had the ambience of a discount shoe store with its linoleum floor, metal shelves, crowded aisles. It wasn't unusual to encounter a dead mouse in a corner trap. The books were stacked vertically in piles, making the lower volumes difficult to retrieve.

The sole concession to the locale was a narrow case near the back with shelves devoted to the work of Horla, the village's one famous contemporary author. Although elderly now, she still lived somewhere nearby and was even seen occasionally, walking with a cane in her bony hand.

Dorn passed the bookshop, went up the street, and turned so that, as always, he would pass the school in the hope that Ravenna might look out her classroom window at the same moment and see him. Then he went home.

Or rather, to his own street, Linder Row, for he had the bag of coffee to deliver. The houses were all identical: extremely narrow, two storeys, pale brick, clay chimneys shaped like rising onions. What differentiated one from the other was the wooden front door, which each inhabitant had painted according to their taste. Red, yellow, green, striped, even polka-dotted and paisley. Dorn could well remember a dispute between Leev's wife and the widow who lived four doors down. Leev's wife had painted their door a particularly attractive shade of blue-grey. And then some three months later the widow had Misoi, the village handyman, paint hers a very similar colour, perhaps just a little more blue. Leev's wife had become indignant. She complained to poor Misoi, who was just doing his job, even as he applied the lacquer finish. The widow herself was away (deliberately?) visiting her sister in the city, and Leev's wife had to wait until she came back. Nevertheless, she knocked on the widow's door. What did she mean by using the same colour? Was it a bad joke? Did she have no respect for a person's right to individuality? And the widow had responded, What nonsense, they aren't anything alike, perhaps you just like my colour more than yours, and so on.

Leev's wife refused to drop the issue. She called a special meeting of the Linder Row house owners and forced them to take a vote. Dorn himself contrived to have a bad cold that day and so did not attend; if he had, the vote would not have been tied. Leev's wife insisted that she would take her complaint to the village council, but not long after that (probably it was a coincidence of timing), she left Leev and moved to the city, becoming one of the many exiles from village life. About a year later, the widow died and the new owners repainted the door a rather unpleasant shade of orange. Leev, now alone, left his own door as it was, the colour of a child's clear and wondering eyes.

Dorn walked up the short path to Leev's house, the pleasant weight of the coffee beans in one hand, his copy of *Vordram* in the other. He used the brass knocker. A commotion behind the door caused him to take a step back: a terrible growling followed by a smack against the other side. Did Leev have a new pet?

"Who's there?"

"It's your neighbour, Dorn."

"Right. Hold on a second."

There were more sounds of scuffling and then Leev's stern voice. The bolt retreated and the door opened, but only a few centimetres. Leev stared with one eye through the gap, blocking the space with his body. Something seemed to be pushing him from behind.

"I'm sorry to be short with you, Dorn, but what is it you want?"

Now whatever it was jerked Leev from one side to the other. Dorn held up the bag. "Your coffee order. I've brought it from the café."

"Ah, good. Been out for two days. Got a splitting headache from caffeine withdrawal."

"I don't think it's going to quite fit through that little gap."

"Hang on, I don't want the animal to get away again. Go on, move back, move back!"

These last words were obviously not addressed to Dorn. After some vigorous shoving, Leev opened the door a few more centimetres, still keeping his body pressed to the now larger gap. Behind him the animal leapt up, barking. Over Leev's shoulder Dorn could now see the dog, large and shaggy but also thin at the ribs. It tried to squeeze its snout between Leev's legs.

"Quick!" Leev commanded, and Dorn thrust the bag forward, allowing his neighbour to pull it into the house.

Just at that moment the dog successfully pushed its head through, and Dorn saw its bloodshot eyes and carnivorous, snapping jaws.

"Go back, I tell you!" Leev gave the creature a hard shove.

"That's quite the pooch you've got," Dorn said, trying to sound light-hearted despite his visceral fear of the animal. "What is it? A shepherd? A husky?"

"It's a wolf, actually."

"Yes, ha ha, why wouldn't it be?"

"No, seriously. It's pure wolf."

"Seriously? I thought that was illegal."

"Used to be. You haven't heard of the new program?"

"What program?"

"Hey," Leev shouted, half turning his head. "Stop that right now." He kicked back a foot, and the wolf—if it was a wolf—yelped and backed away.

"What's that on your arm, Leev? Are those stiches?"

Leev chuckled humourlessly. "Well, it takes a bit to get used to a new roommate, doesn't it?"

"But are you sure you're safe?"

"I don't feel safe driving on the Torvil Expressway, if it comes to that."

"I don't know what to say, Leev. Does he have a name?"

"It's a she, actually. And you're not supposed to name them, it's part of the mystique. Listen, she's got hold of my shirttail. I better go."

"Yes, of course."

"Thanks, Dorn. If you ever want to stop by for a cup—"

A low-throated growl cut him off. Leev's eyes opened wide and he suddenly shut the door. Dorn stood there a moment, listening to the receding sounds. He had known Leev was an oddball, but this really took the cake. Shaking his head, he stepped over the low hedge, a shortcut to his own door.

❧ 4 ❧

Architecture

Dorn had never wanted to go to architecture school, or even to take the entry examination. It was his mother, dying at home, who asked him to. She didn't worry about his brother the way she worried about Dorn's future. To her, Dorn seemed so aimless and withdrawn from the world; what was he possibly going to do with his life?

In the end, Dorn didn't take the examination for his mother. He took it because his father, sitting in the corner armchair, looked up from his bird-racing paper and said, "He'll just fail it, anyway." So he took the exam, barely passed, got put on a waiting list, and received a registered letter announcing his acceptance two days before the start of class.

A duffel bag of unfashionable clothes over his shoulder, Dorn got on the bus, then the train, and moved to the city.

His dormitory roommate, a supposed science major, actually specialized in furtive masturbation; Dorn would be woken in the night by the sound of his squeaking mattress. The school prided itself on a "technical approach to the urban environment," meaning there were no discussions about aesthetics, social housing, or other subjects that might have interested Dorn. Instead, each student was made to buy the eighteen-hundred-page *Compendium of Regulatory Building Statutes* and begin memorizing.

He spent his time hunched over his tiny desk, the enormous book open, trying to remember the allowable distances from door to fire escape or the minimum ventilation requirements for commercial kitchens. He ate alone in the cafeteria while staring out the window into the gymnasium, where young men played Skvirborim.

In one of his classes, there was a girl who attracted Dorn's attention. She wasn't particularly pretty, but he liked the way she curled her loose hair around a finger. Plus she looked as depressed as he felt. Yet he could not summon the courage to approach her, not even on the day she turned her head and absent-mindedly smiled at him.

To alleviate his depression and boredom, Dorn took from under his bed the set of carving tools his uncle had given him. He began to carve the only wood available—his desk. He drew vines and blossoms up the square legs and, getting down on his knees, began to chip and shave and cut. As he carved, he made the flowers more three-dimensional, the vines increasingly detailed. When he reached the top, he began carving a relief image, a recreation of a famous nature painting by Hibil.

On the day Dorn finished his carving, he read in the student paper that a person in his class had attempted suicide by jumping into the library atrium from an upper floor. The person's name was not released, but when he went to class, the girl who curled her hair around her finger was absent. Nor did she appear the next day. Dorn was overcome with grief, although he couldn't tell whether it was for the girl or himself. He knew only that he couldn't bear to remain at school a minute longer and went immediately to the registrar's office to withdraw. Then he returned to his room, packed his duffel bag, and left.

It was upon crossing the main quad of the university, heading towards the bus station, that he saw the girl. She was walking in the other direction, talking to the professor, and looking perfectly well.

✹ 5 ✹

Patriarch

On Saturday morning, Dorn went to visit his father.

The village's old-age home, a faux-rustic building made to look like a hunting lodge, stood next to the river on the northern edge of town, beyond which rose the forest. The home had room for sixty-five residents and was always full. Yet almost as soon as an aging villager began to inquire about a place, it seemed that one resident or another would begin a quick decline. A funeral in one of the three surrounding cemeteries was followed by a small moving van pulling up to the home to disgorge the new resident's token remains of an independent life—an easy chair, a rug and bookcase, perhaps a painting or record player. Dorn's father's room contained all these things, along with an eighteenth-century brass sextant in an oak case, given to him upon retirement from his job as a traffic manager for a shipping company.

Feenis had a private room on the second floor. For an eighty-three-year-old he wasn't in bad shape, despite having had his gall bladder removed and a growth taken from his neck, and his needing a daily heart medication. He could move around well enough with a cane, and his mind was still nimble. Or rather, Dorn would have said, his mouth was still quick with a remark even if his opinions had been carved in stone decades ago.

And yet there had been a most unlikely change in his father's life. Last year Feenis had fallen in love. The object of his affection was a sixty-one-year-old nurse on his floor, a short and stocky woman with a penetrating laugh. The woman had at first joked about the old man's obvious infatuation with her, which had him doing all kinds of unlikely and ridiculous things: writing poems, ordering flowers, breaking out into raspy song—things he had never done for Dorn's mother. And it seemed that even as an old man his father was more successful than Dorn with women, for over time the nurse, name of Torpe, had come to return the feelings, or at least to claim that she didn't mind. Naturally, Dorn had been suspicious, but when he made it clear to her that his father had only his pension, she had laughed and said, "You don't think I know? I'm worth a lot more than that pervy old sod!" Before long, Torpe had moved into the room with him, the only person in residence below the age of seventy-five. Nor did she give up her duties on the floor, but continued to administer to the residents. What his father's private life was now like, Dorn preferred not to imagine. He did know that Torpe kept an air mattress in the closet because Feenis was, in her words, "a terrible thrasher and his toenails could open a vein."

On Saturday Dorn arrived with a large container of Yiss, a brand of infant's vanilla pudding that for some reason his father could not get enough of. One of Dorn's miniatures was displayed in the front bay window of the building, a particularly saccharine scene of a white-haired woman and a bald man, both wearing the casual, light-coloured clothes of the retired, holding hands on an old-fashioned swing that hung from the branch of an apple tree. Dorn went through the automatic door, nodded to the receptionist behind her desk, and crossed the hushed lobby, where several residents sat in plush armchairs, looking at old magazines or staring into space. He took the winding staircase two vigorous steps at a time, as if to prove how far he was from his own move-in date, walked to the end of the hall, and then, as had been his custom for so long, went in without knocking.

On the bed lay his father—hardly unusual, but instead of being asleep he had an urgent, pained expression on his face. Sitting at the end of the bed, her wide body blocking the rest of his father, was the nurse, Torpe. Was she performing her professional duty or satisfying his father in some other way? Dorn retreated into the hall, staying by the door until he heard a strangled gargling sound, waited some more, then knocked before going in.

Torpe was just picking up her knitting from the armchair. His father was sitting up in bed, the strands of his thin comb-over askew.

"Look here, Feenis!" Torpe said. "It's your own true boy, arriving like clockwork to visit the patriarch."

"Did you bring my Yiss?"

"Yes, I'll put it in your fridge."

"It isn't the low-fat kind, is it?"

"I won't make that mistake again."

The small fridge was hidden by a cupboard door. When Dorn opened the fridge, he was surprised to find the shelves stacked with beer. He had to make room for the pudding.

"So, Dorn," the nurse said, "have you thought about my idea?"

"What idea is that?"

"To work for the movies. They use all kinds of miniatures. When they do a pirate picture, they use a miniature pirate ship. When they do an airplane crash, they take a tiny plane and smash it up. And they pay a fortune for every model, I read about it. Don't you agree, Feenis? Your son could do very well."

"Dorn isn't interested in money like his brother. Never has been. What he is interested in I've never been able to figure out."

Dorn told himself not to get riled up. He said, "I don't think they use models anymore. They do everything with computer animation now."

"So you're the expert? Do you read the magazines?" Torpe

asked, and then laughed for reasons Dorn couldn't understand. "Well, I've got to make my rounds, so I'll leave you conspirators alone. I'll be back soon with your pills, Feenis."

"I'm going to eat pudding."

"Pills first!"

The door closed behind her. Dorn felt awkward standing there but didn't want to move the knitting left on the chair. Besides, sitting in the room always made him so drowsy that he'd have to struggle not to close his eyes.

"So how are you?"

"I'm shit," Feenis said. "I'm pure shit."

"What do you mean?"

"Because that's what life is. It's shit. We make it, we stand in it, and we eat it."

"You're not happy with Torpe around? Because I can ask her to leave, you know. You have no obligation to her."

"She'd knock you across the room. Besides, what does it have to do with her? Look at your own pathetic life, Dorn."

"We aren't talking about me just now."

"It's thin as a piece of paper. Thin, thin, thin. Where's the fucking joy?"

"I'm going to check your medications with the doctor."

"What did you even come for? You haven't a single thing to tell me."

"I do, as it happens. You remember my neighbour, Leev? I knocked on his door the other day and discovered that he's now living with a wolf. A real wolf, a wild animal. It's already bitten him. There's some new government program."

"Everyone knows about that program," his father said. "Especially your brother."

"Vin? What does he have to do with it?"

"Come here."

Dorn stepped towards him.

"Come closer. Come on, come on."

Dorn moved up to the bed and, as his father kept gesturing with his crooked hand, leaned forward and then more, until his face was almost beside his father's.

"Not everyone," Feenis whispered softly, putting his hand on Dorn's shoulder. "Not every father can show his affections in the same way."

Then he tipped his head back and began to howl.

⚜ 6 ⚜

Improved

Dorn made a final check of the model for the sex shop, making sure he hadn't missed any details. He got a reinforced cardboard box from the cupboard, put in a layer of foam, picked up the model, and placed it inside. He filled the rest of the box with foam peanuts and fitted on the top.

Behind his house was a tiny strip of garden, identical in size to those of the other houses on Linder Row. Most had modern gas barbecues, narrow flower beds, a couple of patio chairs, and a small table. Dorn's was completely neglected. There was a rectangle of broken flagstones meant as a patio and then overgrown grass and weeds. For some time he'd been meaning to reclaim it so that in good weather he might sit back there with a cold beer and a book, but it remained one of his many unrealized projects. Instead, it was merely the space where he kept his three-wheel delivery tricycle with its large mesh basket.

These foot-pedalled vehicles had once been encouraged by the village council; Dorn had even received a partial grant to buy his. At one time there were quite a few moving through the streets, but now only a handful remained in working order. He'd seen an older woman riding one about a month ago; she'd given a comradely salute.

As he came up to the tricycle, Dorn saw a small orange cat sleeping in the basket. It belonged to a neighbour whose own well-tended garden backed onto Dorn's. For some reason, the cat preferred his yard, using it not just for sleeping but as a litter box. "Go on, shoo," he said, and the cat blinked, stretched lazily, and hopped to the ground. Dorn placed the box in the basket and pulled the trike between the houses towards the street, where he got on and began to pedal. Almost immediately some snub-nosed car came up behind and got uncomfortably close, impatient to pass. Dorn had learned to ignore such drivers and he kept an even pace, enjoying the strenuous motions of his legs and then gliding along a road that curved down to the main street. He passed a billboard bolted to the side of a brick building, turning his head to read it.

BRING THE WILD HOME
Obtain your animal licence today from the Village Hall—
be part of this exciting pilot project!

How long had it been there? Weren't billboards banned by order of a village by-law? He couldn't understand why he seemed to be learning about this program after everyone else and saw it as another sign that life was somehow passing him by. He tried to imagine bringing some wild creature into his house—after all, he lived alone like Leev. Perhaps a little companionship and responsibility would do him good. But he'd never even owned a hamster; his otherwise indulgent mother had forbidden pets, caring more for her porcelain figurines, which populated every table and shelf. As a result, Dorn was slightly afraid of both dogs and cats, an embarrassment he tried to hide by making an excess show of appreciating other people's animals.

He reached the sex shop and pulled up to the curb. There was no need to lock his trike—not because the village was crime-free but because nobody would want it. The shop was, either ironically or practically, next to the maternity clothing store. Tul and Tule, the owners, certainly hadn't tried to be tasteful or artistic in how they filled the gingerbread house–like window. They had simply built a pyramid of products: sex toys, clothing, lubricants, and boxes of tentacled prophylactics.

Tul and Tule were both about sixty, with weathered skin and identical silver crewcuts. They were not a couple but brother and sister, although years ago there had been rumours—without the slightest evidence, as far as Dorn knew—of an incestuous relationship. One day, people winked, Tule would give birth to a baby with three eyes or some mental defect. This sort of talk passed the time in a village.

He picked up the box and was just reaching the door when it opened and a man with a straw hat pulled low over his face came out. He held the door open, keeping his head down, but although Dorn had never spoken to the man, he recognized him as Mair, a teacher at the same school as Ravenna. In fact, Ravenna had once mentioned in an offhand way that she and Mair had dated for a while and it hadn't ended well.

Inside the store, Dorn made his way to the counter and lowered the box. As if they had been hiding, first Tul and then Tule popped up.

"Hello there, Dorn," Tul said. "We were just checking on inventory. Getting low on butt plugs, aren't we, Tule? I see you've finished the model. How exciting! Let's have a look-see."

"Of course," Dorn said. He took a retractable knife from his pocket to cut the tape and removed the top. He lifted the model out, gently shaking off the foam pieces, and placed it on the counter.

"Aw, it's the sweetest!" cried Tule. "Do you see, Tul? Look at the man's wee boner. And the smile on his face. Marvellous!"

"And those nipples," said Tul, nodding. "They're A1. You've done a splendid job. Here, we've got your money all ready to go." He opened the old-fashioned cash register and, taking out a manila envelope, handed it to Dorn.

"Have a cookie," Tule said. "I just baked them." She held out a plate, and Dorn, who had a sweet tooth, took one. Only as he was moving it towards his mouth did he notice that it was in the shape of a cock and balls.

"Why don't you look around?" Tul said. "You might see something you like. We could give you a discount."

"I don't have that much time today," Dorn said as he chewed. "Maybe another day."

"You're still living alone, yes?"

"Last time I checked."

"Tule, show him the doll."

"Good idea. She's a lovely thing. It's amazing how they've improved."

"I don't really—"

But Tule was already taking something from a box and pressing a button so that the doll started to inflate. It looked disturbingly childlike, with pasted-on bangs, a round face, and a mouth in an open O.

"A lot of bachelors are picking them up," Tul said.

"And women, too," Tule added. "Plus, we've now got males, if you're so inclined. They have a special button to get their members stiff. No flagging with one of those."

"Certified non-toxic," said Tul, "Sniff her, Dorn. The old ones used to smell like an inflatable lifeboat."

Dorn thanked them quickly and got out of there, blushingly aware of his prudish temperament. He certainly believed that people should be allowed to do whatever they liked, as long as nobody was being hurt by it. As he began to pedal down the street, he tried to imagine being attracted to the idea of bonking a rubber doll. If that was possible, then he must have been even more alienated from his desires than he knew. Despite himself, pedalling harder, Dorn couldn't help remembering his last sexual encounter.

It had been three months after his girlfriend left, at the end of a particularly bleak winter day. Dorn hadn't gone out or even spoken to another human being on the phone for at least two days. To prevent himself from drinking too much, he had put on his sheepskin boots, down jacket, hat, and scarf, and forced himself to take a walk.

The temperature had been punishing. Sudden gusts penetrated his clothes. He walked bent over, gloved hands thrust into his pockets, boots leaving prints in the last dusting of snow. He had only a vague sense of where he was going, and before too long he was on an unfamiliar street of narrow three-storey row houses. The end of his nose, painful a moment ago, had grown numb so that he began to worry about frostbite. And then he had noticed the pink flame in a third-floor window.

It wasn't really a flame but an electric bulb, the sign of a prostitute. Sex workers plied their trade in a legal grey area due to the government's reluctance to choose sides on the issue, especially considering how it divided the women's rights groups. These days most such workers filed tax returns and followed the rules of a semi-official regulating body, which included health checks and provisions for welfare and safety.

Dorn convinced himself that wanting to get out of the cold was his prime motivation for walking up to the door and pressing the bell. He heard the buzzer of the lock and went into a tiny vestibule that led to a steep and narrow stairway wallpapered in an unlikely pattern of cowboys and horses. Thumping up in his boots, he felt equal amounts of stimulation and dread, as if he were about to prove there was no purpose to this existence beyond the excitement of humiliation. The door opened even before he knocked, and he went inside.

The light was low and the air smelled pleasantly of incense, not unlike the therapeutic massage studio he occasionally visited. "Come inside, you must be freezing," said a woman in a high, girlish voice, and he began to take off his winter things before getting a look at her. She took his hand—he saw dark hair, a soft-looking neck, and a waist a little thick—and led him into a bedroom decorated in the expected reds and purples, with a shag carpet and plenty of pillows.

She sat on the edge of the bed. "What's your name?"

"Dorn."

"I'm Koj. I didn't think I'd see anybody out on a night like this. It's been quiet for days."

"I was just taking a walk to get some air. I didn't intend..."

"Why don't you sit down beside me. And you don't have to avert your eyes. I like to be looked at."

He did as he was told. She had a nice round face, though she was certainly older than he was. Her hair was likely dyed, and he suspected she'd had a bit of work done around her eyes and mouth.

"You don't need to worry. This is for you to enjoy. I gather it's been a while."

"Yes. My girlfriend left me."

"We don't want to bring her into the room, now do we?" She reached out and brushed her fingers across his lips. "Do you have anything in mind?"

"No, nothing. Should I pay now?"

"For nothing?" She laughed lightly. "Yes, if you don't mind. Is that your wallet? I'll take these two bills out, all right? I think the best thing would be for you to relax while I make you feel good. Why don't you take your clothes off and lie down on the bed."

Again he obeyed, although he was self-conscious of the pallor of his skin, the slight bulge of his waist, and the skinniness of his legs. His head propped on the pillows, he was able to see her undress, which she did as a kind of show, a slightly jokey yet arousing Dance of the Seven Veils. She got onto the bed beside him and pushed her breasts to his face, then moved slowly down, rubbing them on his chest and stomach and over his erection. She slipped him into her mouth.

He made an involuntary noise and closed his eyes. She ran her hands along his thighs and up to his chest and really got down to work. Even in great arousal, he became fearful that he would lose his erection, so he reached down to stroke her hair as if she were someone he cared for. But she pulled away, saying, "Sorry, I have a really sensitive scalp," and as she resumed, he tried to focus on what she was doing. Only, his thoughts kept strangely drifting off—to a camping trip his family had once taken, to a time at architecture school when he had misunderstood the weight-bearing properties of glass brick—and he had to keep bringing his attention back, the way one might pull at the string of a helium balloon. Still, before long he was climaxing into, as it turned out, the rubber he hadn't realized she'd slipped onto him.

Dorn stopped pedalling and coasted to a stop. He hadn't been at all aware of where he was going, but as it turned out he had been taking one of his alternate routes and now faced Silk Park. He was breathing heavily, either from the memory or the steady incline. In the park he could see people performing—somewhat ineptly—various acrobatic feats. An older man juggled several balls, missing one every few beats and having to start over again. Two teenagers watched a third walk across a slackline tied between two trees. The slackline walker teetered back and forth, flapped her hands, then tumbled off. One woman performed a series of neat moves with a hula hoop, twirling it up her body, and then her raised arm, tossing it to a foot, all quite graceful and balletic. A tall woman was watching her. Only when the tall woman took the hoop did Dorn realize it was Ravenna.

Ravenna twirled the hoop and then kept it up with vigorous if awkward gyrations. She started to bring it higher, but instead of moving to her hand, the hoop smacked her on the nose. She cried out and immediately bent forward, holding her nose and both laughing and groaning while the hoop settled at her feet. Just then she looked up and saw Dorn sitting on his trike, watching. Immediately he looked away, but she could hardly mistake him for anyone else on that three-wheeled contraption, and after handing the hoop back she ran towards him while still rubbing her nose.

"Did you really have to witness my moment of humiliation?"

Wearing an old T-shirt and saggy shorts, damp under the arms, she was slightly out of breath. He could just smell her sweat, which brought her physically closer. He said, "I certainly couldn't have done any better. It must take a while to get the hang of it. But what is this, exactly?"

"It's called Circus Fit. Really, it's just another way to exercise. I was getting stupidly bored at the gym. The hoop is actually a lot of fun, even if it is harder than it looks. I just hope none of my students see me. That would be even worse than you."

"I'm impressed by how you try new things. You're adventurous."

"Maybe you're just not restless like me. You like your life the way it is."

If only that were true. He said, "Speaking of new things, do you know about this program to live with a wild animal?"

"Of course. The kids have been excited about it for months."

"That long?"

"They've all been scheming to get their parents into it. In fact, one of them—a pushy boy named Kohool—just succeeded. This week his family took in a female raccoon and three pups, or whatever you call them. And the mother's really big. Kohool gleefully reported that the house is a disaster. The raccoons have learned to open drawers and rip open packages. All they want to eat are cookies."

"Sounds very unpleasant."

"And the three-year-old daughter is terrified of them. She won't stop crying. Personally, I'm allergic to fur, so mammals are out. And I don't think I'm going to put a trout in the bathtub. Actually, I am glad you came by, because I've been thinking. How would you like to visit my class for Professions Day?"

"Me?"

"You could talk about how you became a model maker. There isn't a kid who doesn't know your work. You'd be a big hit."

"I've never given any kind of talk."

"You'll be great at it. Agreed?"

A shout came from the park. The woman instructor was waving Ravenna's hoop at her.

"Uh-oh, look what you've done. Now I'm in trouble! I'm thrilled you're coming to my class."

She startled him with a sweaty hug and then turned and tripped before laughing again and running away.

A New Order

One morning, when he went to retrieve the newspaper, Dorn found an envelope that had been pushed halfway through the mail slot. Halfway because the envelope was stuffed full and had become jammed. He carefully worked it out and read the shaky printing on it: *To Dorn, Model Maker.*

He took the envelope back to the table where his milky coffee and rusks and cheese awaited. When he opened it, a fan of bills sprang out. He laid them aside to unfold the letter. It was written with the same shaky letters, as if someone had been trying to disguise their handwriting.

Master Builder Dorn,
I wish you to make for me a model. It is to be a building of your own choice. And it is to be on fire. On the top floor

there is to be a figure visible in the window. A figure that knows it cannot escape.

I am convinced that you have the skill and talent to depict such a scene. Enclosed please find half the fee. You shall receive as much again upon completion and will be contacted with instructions for delivery.

If you do not wish to accept this commission, you need only leave the envelope back on your doorstep. However, I sincerely hope you do. It will bring me much pleasure.

Sincerely yours.

There was no name or signature. Now Dorn counted the money, almost a third more than half his usual fee. The thought of making a model of a burning building did not particularly appeal to him. He was well aware of his own squeamishness: he avoided violent movies, disliked how gruesome the costumes for Halloween had become, and if there was ever a police car or ambulance nearby, he did not stroll over to gawk, afraid of what he might see. On the other hand, he hadn't received any work since finishing the sex shop model and could hardly be choosy. And on the plus side, most of his commissions were for interior scenes. The challenge of creating the façade of a building did, on second thought, intrigue him.

The telephone rang. Dorn had no cellphone, and his land line rang so infrequently that Dorn always jumped at the sound. He picked up the receiver and heard the voice of his brother.

"Dorn?"

"What's the matter? Is Father ill?"

"I've got something to show you. If you wouldn't mind coming over."

"Right now?"

"I'll see you shortly, then."

His brother never said goodbye but simply hung up, one of his unconscious acts of aggression. But what could Dorn do about that, or about being summoned as if he were a servant? Although younger by eleven months, Vin had been more successful on the playground, in school, with girls, and in business. Their pattern had long ago been set. Whenever Vin threw a stick, it was Dorn's duty to fetch it.

To say that Dorn and Vin were different was like comparing a mid-winter afternoon to a summer storm. As a child, Dorn had rarely cried or demanded but sat watching the world with melancholy eyes that inspired adults to say he had been born with an old soul. His brother, on the other hand, was a thumper, a screamer, a thrower of food and toys. Dorn accepted the rules of the world; Vin remade them to suit his whims. Dorn grew to the country's exact average for male height, while Vin turned out short, stocky, and powerful. He excelled at sports that demanded cunning and tenacity. For a time he was their school's champion wrestler, until it was discovered that he was occasionally betting on himself to lose.

Dorn had a series of typical interests as a boy: birdwatching, rockhounding, and then carving. Vin developed an interest only in ambition itself. He told Dorn that he always wanted to be "head of the pack," "respected," and even someone "other people are afraid of." Too impatient to finish a business degree, he plunged into the financial world of the city and made a lot of money doing what he hinted sometimes crossed the line of legality. "Look, it's simple," he'd said during one of his infrequent visits home. "I take other people's money and move it from one place to another, from cash to commodity, all the while shaving off a nice slice for myself."

Vin always came home driving a new sports car, only to show his annoyance when Dorn confessed to never having heard of the manufacturer. And then one night after midnight the telephone rang. "Guess what, MuMu?"

"I hate it when you call me that," Dorn said drowsily. MuMu was a particularly hapless cartoon character they had watched as children. Vin had called him that at school one day, and the nickname had stuck for years.

"But you still are MuMu. Listen, I'm moving back. That's right, I've developed a hankering for the old hometown. As it turns out, there's a new prestige building just opening up, and I've nabbed the penthouse suite."

Did Vin really want to come back or had some business affair gone wrong, forcing him into retreat? Whatever the reason, three days later Vin returned. The building he had spoken of turned out to be three kilometres downriver from the village. It had been their mother's favourite picnic spot when they were kids, which made Dorn suspect that his brother had something to do with the land sale. The building was a modernist box, as aesthetically alien to the village sensibility as was possible. It had sliding glass doors and a concrete lobby floor with a doorman standing behind a brushed steel counter, a row of video screens behind him showing the feeds from various security cameras.

Perhaps his brother had wanted to literally bulldoze the memory of those family picnics. Now one could eat in the village's only Michelin-rated restaurant, a criminally expensive place at the back of the ground floor. The second floor was occupied by professional offices—a dermatologist, a plastic surgeon, a spa. Strangely, Dorn never encountered anyone who actually lived in the apartments other than his brother, giving him the eerie impression that they were empty.

He always felt ridiculous riding his trike when not out on delivery, but the building was too far to walk. He left it at the back of the building, near the restaurant. Dorn had completed the restaurant's model almost two years ago, a quaint outdoor café scene with a man at a table holding an espresso cup in one hand and a croissant in the other while sparrows the size of teardrops pecked around his feet. It was one of his most charming models, but the management, obviously having felt obliged to order one, had relegated it to a dark alcove between the toilets.

The building's smoked-glass doors opened with a soft whoosh, and Dorn entered the lobby. Despite having seen Dorn several times before, the doorman showed no sign of recognition as he silently turned the visitor's book around. The page for the day was blank. Dorn wrote his name and went to the elevator, which took him swiftly to the penthouse floor. Here there was only one door, a small antique table beside it adorned with a porcelain vase and a single rose. He pressed the buzzer and waited an annoyingly long time (Vin liked to keep him waiting) before the door opened to reveal his hairy-legged brother in a short silk robe.

"Dorn! That was quick. You must have pedalled like mad on that sporty trike of yours."

"And you're not dressed. It seems a little late to be getting up."

"Don't just stand there like you're holding pamphlets offering eternal salvation. Which reminds me of that pathetic religious phase you had as a kid. You even talked about becoming a monk. Funny thing is, in a way you did."

Vin grinned to show it was a joke, but Dorn winced. He saw himself as a sixteen-year-old, sitting cross-legged on the shaggy throw rug at the foot of his bed among copies of the Koran, the Bhagavad Gita, the New Testament, and a compilation of Talmudic wisdom. It was half pretentiousness, half loneliness, and it lasted about two months.

As Dorn came into the sunken living room, he noticed on the glass coffee table a bottle of expensive Telft liquor, made from tiny green berries found only on a certain vine in the northern forest. An enormous TV screen was turned mutely to the financial channel.

"It doesn't look like anything urgent is going on."

"Who said it was urgent? I'm not an emergency room doctor. Let's sit down."

Vin wore his hair almost shoulder length, even now that it was receding at the front. He splayed out on the white leather sofa, and Dorn took up a matching chair, averting his eyes from his brother's exposed genitals. "Have you seen Dad lately?" asked Dorn. "He's still with the nurse Torpe. I really don't know what to think about it."

"Yes, yes, I've been meaning to go. My schedule's been a real bitch lately. But as far as I'm concerned, Dad can get his rocks off with whoever he—"

At that moment a woman walked in from the bedroom. It was like a scene from a film, the woman in only a long T-shirt. It took Dorn a second to recognize her as one of the tellers at the bank. She didn't return his uncomfortable smile but merely picked up some clothes strewn on the floor.

"You're not going, are you?" Vin said without bothering to look at her.

"Fuck you, Vin."

"If you're lucky," his brother said, raising his eyebrows. The teller went out the apartment door, the bundle of clothes in her arms.

"I know you're wondering how I do it," Vin said with a sly look.

"I'm not wondering at all. It seems perfectly clear to me."

"I tell you, Dorn, it's not about money and it's certainly not about looks. It's all about how a person presents himself to the world. Whether he looks like someone who can take what he wants. I've always thought that you had far more appealing attributes than me. You're taller, not half bad-looking, and have that sad-dog face that a lot of women find irresistible. If only you didn't slouch when you walked, and looked people in the eye, and raised your voice above a whisper—"

"I know you mean well," Dorn interrupted him. "But I didn't come here for life advice."

"How do you know I mean well? I could be screwing you over. See? You're too trusting. By the way, what about that scarecrow of a teacher you like? Ravenna. Have you banged her yet?"

"Please don't talk like that. I wish I hadn't said anything about her. That's the last time I go drinking with you."

"You do know that these days fourteen-year-olds are getting laid. Most boys get their first blow job on the school bus. And here you are, all huffy like I've sullied her honour. You want to challenge me to a duel?"

Dorn sighed. "Why is it that we can't have a normal conversation? I'm going to leave."

He rose. So did Vin.

"Listen, Dorn. I know we can be like oil and water, but you've always been a good brother. And let's not forget that it's me who pays Dad's extra bills."

"No, you never do let me forget."

"The point is, I have a small favour to ask. It's nothing, really." Vin went over to a wall of glass shelves. There were a few expensive-looking trinkets but no books. He picked up a small, rectangular box and brought it over.

"Here," Vin said, holding it out.

Dorn took the box. It was quite beautiful marquetry work, with a complex geometrical pattern inlaid around the top. Dorn guessed it to be mid-eighteenth century.

"I want you to keep this for me," Vin said.

"What's inside it?"

"Nothing you need to worry about."

"For how long?"

"Until I need it back. It's hardly much of a favour."

"Yes, all right."

"Thanks, Dorn," Vin said in a voice like a character from a cowboy movie. "You're a real pal."

Just then something made Dorn jump. An animal, dark and sleek, raced out from under the sofa towards him, veering at the last moment to slip under a closet door.

"What in the world was that?"

Vin grinned. "Oh, that's just my mink."

"Your what?"

"From the Wild Home Project. They approved me right away; it helps when they know you at the village council. I thought of getting something bigger, but a mink seemed like an animal the ladies might like. It's been a little disappointing, to be honest. Hides most of the time."

"Do you have something to do with the project? Dad seemed to think so."

Vin shrugged. "If there's money to be made, I don't see why some of it shouldn't come to me. Let's not mention a certain forestry operation, or a transportation company, or—"

"Is this another attempt to log the forest? I thought that was permanently outlawed."

"What's really permanent in this world? Not you or me, brother. Hey, want to see the mink again? Watch this, it's very cool."

Vin walked past the counter that separated the living room from the large modern kitchen. He opened the mirrored door of the refrigerator and from a tub took out a strip of meat. Liver, it looked like to Dorn.

"Want to hold it?" Vin asked, holding out the glistening piece.

"No, thank you."

Vin crouched down and stretched out his hand. "Come here, darling mink, time for your iron supplement."

In seconds the mink's nose poked out from under the closet door. Then it came on a run, snapping and snarling. It stopped about a metre before Vin, body pressed to the ground, black eyes staring up, splendid tail sweeping the floor. Then, almost faster than one could follow, it leapt up to grab the liver, taking off again.

"Jesus!" Vin cried. "I thought for a moment I was going to lose my left ball."

"Why do you even want an animal here?"

"If I asked myself that all the time, I'd never buy anything. Put that box in a safe place, Dorn."

"I will," Dorn said, moving towards the door. "But if I were you, Vin, I'd put my balls in a safe place."

❧ 8 ❧

Watering Hole

If Dorn were to bring a wild animal into his house, what sort would it be? A jackrabbit, perhaps, or a mildly venomous snake? But no matter how seriously he searched himself, he couldn't find even a hint of such desire. If it was just his brother, Vin, that would be one thing, but it was also Leev, and Ravenna's pupil, and presumably a lot of others, too.

It seemed important that he try to understand. Perhaps behind this strange need was the same emotion that had people sighing at snow-capped mountains or bulrushes waving in a marsh. A romantic longing for nature, a living world untouched by human intervention. Rows of growing corn or the sight of cows behind a fence staring at one's passing car only proved how we had put a collar and leash on the wildness we ourselves had emerged from.

He wasn't convinced by his own philosophizing. Maybe it was simply the creatures themselves. After all, like most children, Dorn himself had loved anything to do with animals. He had a folder of animal pictures cut from magazines; he was fascinated by nature documentaries. A wild animal's perfection had nothing whatsoever to do with the human gaze—it existed beyond and outside of people.

But if that was so, why did people want to possess one? Unless *possess* was the wrong word. Leev was the only real example Dorn had—he dismissed his brother's motivation as being the usual greedy hunger for status. He wondered if it had anything to do with Leev's wife leaving, an apparently traumatizing event that had left him weeping in his tiny back garden. But surely Leev couldn't believe that he truly owned that wolf in his house. Something had loosened in Leev, or had revealed itself, a kind of wildness in his own being. The best he might imagine was that he was living in parallel with the wolf, like two different species sharing a watering hole and giving each other wary glances as they drank.

"Bullshit," Dorn said aloud to himself, going to the fridge for another beer. "Or possibly bullshit."

⚜ 9 ⚜

Author

As a tourist destination, the village was known for its quaintness, for the steam-powered clock whose metallic figures paraded on the hour in front of the village hall, for Dorn's models (a not-quite-up-to-date walking guide was available at the hall), for a kind of cheese—similar to blue but even stronger, a match for the local brown ale—and for its proximity to the forest. But there was another reason, the only one that had given it any international renown. The village was the residence of the author Horla.

Horla hadn't always stayed here but had returned to the village some thirty years ago. At the time she gave a rather notorious newspaper interview in which she said, "The simple truth is that, despite the pretty trappings, our country is corrupt to its core. And no place is more corrupt than its villages.

Since I cannot get away from this festering, I have no choice but to sink into its maggoty heart."

Not surprisingly, her words did not endear her to the local inhabitants, who considered themselves perfectly decent people. For years she was grumbled about and even resented for refusing to socialize or at least make some public appearances. Only rarely would she be sighted walking in the forest or along the river, an upright, elderly woman with flowing white hair and a wooden staff in her hand. Even in summer she wore a man's vest, wool trousers, heavy shoes. But time does its work and people began to feel differently. The village became known as the place where the great author Horla lived. After she donated her papers to the small Ushla College (not technically in the village but close enough), scholars began to make pilgrimages, staying in guesthouses, eating in the restaurants. The only thing Horla was said to like about the village was the cheese and ale, and all three taverns declared themselves her preferred watering hole.

Before the author's arrival, the bookshop did not stock even her latest book. She was hardly the sort of writer favoured by villagers, who preferred gruesome mysteries and farcical novels about civil servants. In the first year after her arrival, the bookshop showed its solidarity with the residents by continuing to ignore her. But in time, visitors began to enquire, and the simple fact is that no bookshop can afford to miss a sale. So the owner ordered her latest, published by the same alternative press that had first discovered her, a book that matched her others with its black cover, white type, and small, blurry photograph in the centre. But visitors didn't want only the latest; they asked for Horla's other works. And so two or three more titles were carried, and then more, until all her books could be seen displayed on dedicated shelves along one narrow wall. There were even a few early journal appearances and rare first editions in a glass case. Whereas other small bookshops relied on guides and cookbooks to stay afloat, the village's bookshop survived thanks to the works of Horla.

As to what sort of writer she was, the answer even from her admirers had to be: a difficult one. Her detractors called her work misanthropic muck. Although each novel was as slim as a poetry book, many readers had a hard time finishing even one. The books were a remarkably uniform lot, with names like *Inhabit*, *After Interrogation*, and *Putrescence*, written in a first-person confessional voice or with an unnamed but complicit narrator. There might be some sort of action in the early or late pages, even violence, but the rest would be rumination, recrimination, accusation, and emotional self-flagellation. The novels had been translated into some thirty languages and were studied in dozens of university courses. Every year hers was among the names offered for the Nobel Prize, but the rumour was that one juror, a former lover from half a century ago, always blackballed her. Horla's own attitude towards the prize was unknown, for she had stopped giving interviews after her second book.

It was a sign in the bookshop window that alerted Dorn to a highly improbable event: the publication of her first book for children. Horla herself, the sign announced, had done the pictures. The name of the book was *The Blinking Eye*.

More astonishing still was a second sign stating that the book would be available exclusively at the village bookshop on tomorrow's publication day and that Horla herself would be present to sign copies.

Dorn knew that signed copies of her books were extremely hard to come by. He wondered whether the author could have developed an affection for the village or a desire to help the bookshop, which she had apparently never entered. But even people who couldn't stand her work would understand how valuable these copies would become. As for Dorn, he was an admirer of Horla, at least the three slim novels he had managed to get through. And he had a particular fondness for children's books; it was a subject he and Ravenna often talked about. Perhaps one day Dorn would have a child of his own. Surely one of the great pleasures of parenthood would be reading aloud. And so, on the day in question, Dorn hung up his apron early and headed towards the main street to get in line at the bookshop.

The afternoon was particularly beautiful, the air sweet, the branches overhead filled with song. While on his way, Dorn looked up and saw a long-legged Stilt-Walker rebuilding its perennial nest in a chimney. There were fewer now, but when he was a child almost every house had its family of these ungainly birds, and there was an oft-told joke that every villager would be shat upon three times in their life—once as a child, once in middle life, and once just before death.

Already a line-up had formed at the bookshop. It snaked out the open door and along the main street for three blocks before someone had thought to turn up a side street. No doubt it would have been four, five, or even ten times longer if word had gotten out earlier. Even so, Dorn heard several languages being spoken by admirers who had somehow managed to get here.

He joined the line at the end, prepared to wait dutifully for an hour or even more. "Well, hello, stranger," called a voice, and he looked ahead to see Ravenna five or six ahead of him, easy to spot as she was taller than everyone around her. As always when he saw her, his heart—or whatever it was that felt like his heart—did a sort of flip in his chest. Seeing her unexpectedly felt like a gift from the powers above, even if he didn't believe in any such powers.

"Don't tell me you're a Horla fan, too!" she said.

"I am. Some of her work, at least."

"Funny that she's never come up in conversation. I don't know who I hate more after I read one of her books, myself or civilization as a whole. Just don't tell me that you understood *The Curl of the Wave*. Because I'll have to hit you with my shoe."

"I couldn't get ten pages into that one."

"But *Mended Glass*! I cried for an hour after I finished it and didn't even know why."

"Excuse me," said the man behind her, "but you're leaning into me."

"Well, sorry!" She gave Dorn a comical look. "Hey, join me up here?"

No doubt anyone else would have, but Dorn was incapable of jumping ahead in a line. "That's all right. I better stay here."

"Fine. It's a good thing I brought some work." From her bag she pulled out her student folder and drew a pencil from behind her ear.

He sighed regretfully and settled back in line. By now there were a dozen people behind him. It felt better, somehow, not being the very last.

They waited a half-hour. The line grew longer. Another half-hour. People began to grumble. The man in front of Dorn shook his head and walked away. A woman left, and when the couple in front of him drifted off, Dorn ended up just two from Ravenna. She put away the folder.

"Isn't this just like Horla," she said. "Perhaps it's even a trick and she's not coming at all. Perhaps there's not even a children's book. I mean, it does seem impossible that she'd write one. I read somewhere that she dislikes kids."

"How would they know, when she never gives interviews?"

"Good point."

"Do you want to leave?" Dorn asked. Suddenly the prospect of going off with Ravenna struck him as more attractive than getting some book.

"That's the sick thing," she said. "The longer you stand here, investing your time, the harder it is to leave. We should have taken off forty minutes ago, but now I can't do it."

Ten minutes later, an announcement from the shop owner moved through the line. Horla had been delayed by a minor accident. Apparently an animal of some kind, part of the Wild Home Project, had got out an open window and knocked her down. The word was that she had an ankle sprain or bruised wrist. She would be here soon, and in the meantime the store was going to begin selling books to speed things up. A person could purchase a copy and then rejoin the line at the end. When everyone had gone through the process, the first customer in line would be at the front again.

The line began to move. They shuffled a step forward, waited, and shuffled again. It was a full hour before Dorn got into the bookstore, another few minutes until he handed a bill to the cashier, pocketed his change, and picked up his copy of *The Blinking Eye*. He had only time to look at the cover—the title in plain black letters and underneath an almost round eyeball, complete with lid and lashes, drawn with what looked like black marker. Then he was following the person ahead of him, back along the line on the main street and up the side street until he was at the end again. But either there had been some jostling or others had left with unsigned books, because now Dorn found himself beside Ravenna.

"We meet at last," Dorn said boldly.

"How do you do, kind sir? I'm dying to read this. Shall we?"

"Definitely."

Together they opened their books, and, turning slightly away from each other, they read.

❦ 10 ❧

The Blinking Eye

At the beginning of the story, a large eye is resting in the middle of the road.

A school bus moving down the road has to swerve in order not to hit it. Children pour out of the bus.

They surround the eye.

"Football!"

A boy picks up the eye with both hands, and the children run to a nearby playing field.

The eye is much larger than a regular ball, but the children kick it back and forth.

Only one girl doesn't play. She watches sadly from the sidelines.

"Goal!"

The eye blinks.

A long black limousine pulls up. A chauffeur comes around to open the door for a man in a black suit.

The man gives each of the kids a coin. He instructs the chauffeur to pick the eye up and put it in the limousine.

The chauffeur pushes and pushes, but the eye won't fit through the door. So he straps the eye onto the roof.

The eye blinks.

The limousine drives away.

The girl hops on her skateboard.

Through the winding streets of the town they go, and into the hills. At the top of a hill is a factory. There is a sign on the roof: XOP!

The chauffeur opens the door for the man in the black suit, who instructs him to bring in the eye.

The chauffeur, carrying the eye, follows the man inside. The girl slips in behind them.

The man instructs the chauffeur to place the eye high atop a metal ladder. From there the eye can see the workers at their machines below. The man and the chauffeur leave.

The workers work. *Clack, hiss, grind, clack.*

The eye blinks.

One worker stops. He walks up to the ladder and shakes his fist at the eye.

The other workers stop. They shake their fists.

The first worker begins to shake the ladder. Others join him.

The eye wobbles one way and another.

It bounces down the ladder, one step at a time, and rolls

along the factory floor. The girl rushes forward and picks up the eye. It's large enough to almost hide her. She jumps onto her skateboard and rolls out the delivery door just as it opens.

The girl skateboards to a small house.

She just manages to squeeze the eye inside. She takes it upstairs and puts it among the stuffed animals on her bed.

The girl is called for supper.

The eye blinks.

A dog noses its way into the room.

It sees the eye. It growls. It bares its teeth.

The girl rushes in, picks up the eye, and carries it out of the house.

On the street a man is selling balloons.

The girl buys five balloons.

With difficulty she ties the strings around the eye.

She holds up the eye. The balloon begins to lift her and the eye off the ground.

The girl, weeping, lets go.

The eye keeps going. Up, up, blinking into the sky.

River

As Dorn closed the book, he heard a man in line speak out.

"I'm sure not reading this to my kid."

"Beautiful," said a young woman. "And profound."

"You call that profound? Pretentious is more like it."

Dorn looked at Ravenna. She cocked her head and said, so that only he could hear her: "I'm reserving judgment."

"That seems wise."

Another announcement moved down the line. Horla was not coming to sign books after all. Whether her withdrawal was because of the injury, or whether the injury was a made-up excuse, became the subject of debate even as the crowd broke up.

"Well, the weather's nice, anyway," Ravenna said. "And it's Saturday. Want to go for a walk?"

"Yes, I do," said Dorn.

"Just don't blink at me."

"I'm not sure I can help that. We could head for the river."

"That's just what I was thinking."

For Dorn, who didn't like crowds and avoided parades and the like, it was a relief to get away from the near mob of disgruntled book buyers. It took them twenty minutes to reach the river, walking a little apart, occasionally veering towards each other until they brushed shoulders and moved away again. Like a teenager, Dorn was conscious of her hand by his and longed to take it. Except that most teenagers these days had far more courage than he had.

The grass along the village side of the riverbank was newly mown, and benches were placed for optimum views of the gently moving water. On the other bank, wildflowers and weeds grew, turning into prickly bushes and then the first trees of the forest. Generations of village children had been warned not to stray on their own for fear of bogs, poison plants, snakes, and lurking molesters.

Dorn asked, "Have you ever thought of writing a children's book? You have so much experience with kids."

"Me? I spend enough time at a desk or trying to get kids to pay attention. In my free time I want to be hiking or skiing or taking salsa lessons. We're physical beings, not just brains, and I need to move."

"You take salsa lessons?"

"All right, no, but I've thought about it. There's dancing every Thursday night at the community centre. You don't have to go with a partner, but I kind of get creeped out at the thought of being paired up with some old drooler. But if a friend wanted to come, hint hint, that would be different."

"I have two left feet."

"And I have two right. We'd make a perfect couple."

Her tone was joking, but she seemed serious. Salsa dancing was the last thing he would choose to do, unless it was with Ravenna. Could he say something—something to show how he felt?

He gathered his courage and said, "To me it would be better to step on each other's toes than to be in anybody else's arms."

She said nothing, didn't even seem to register what he said, so perhaps his words had been too obscure. Her brow furrowed and she pointed ahead of them. "Is that a police car?"

Dorn looked in the same direction. Yes, it clearly was a police car, driven across the grass and pulled up beside the river. Yellow police tape, the kind one saw on television shows, was stretched between the car, a bench, and a pylon set on the grass. As they watched, a small police boat came burbling up the river.

"This is intriguing," Ravenna said. "Let's go over and look."

"Hmm. Are you sure you want to?"

"My natural curiosity screams yes. Come on."

She grabbed his hand the way a kid might do to pull a friend towards the swings and hurried him along until they got close enough to see something on the triangle of grass defined by the yellow tape. It was a human form, covered by a blanket.

"Oh no," Ravenna whispered.

A policeman stopped writing in his notebook and looked up at them. He walked over, saying, "Would you back away, please. This is a possible crime scene."

"Oh my God, is that a body under there?" Ravenna asked.

"I'm not at liberty to say."

Dorn said, "Is that you, Boolnap? From fifth form?"

The officer looked into Dorn's face. "Dorn?"

"I haven't seen you since graduation. So this is what happened to you."

"Well, my old man was a cop, you know."

"That sounds familiar, now that you mention it."

"I probably never said anything. Back then I was ashamed. In our school, the fathers were all lawyers and doctors."

"Not mine," Dorn said. "This is my friend, Ravenna."

"The teacher, yes? My boy is supposed to be in your class next year."

"Oh, how nice," Ravenna said, not sounding very interested. "So tell us what's what. Is it a murder?"

"If it is, it's a very strange one. A man named Leev."

"Leev? About fifty or fifty-five? Short beard?"

"You know him?"

"He's my neighbour."

"*Was* your neighbour."

"That's terrible. I just knocked on his door the other day. You said a crime scene. Then it really was murder."

"How else does a man have his throat torn out?"

"Ugh, that's hideous." Ravenna made a face.

"So he was a friend of yours, eh, Dorn? The detective might want to speak to you."

"Not a friend, a neighbour. He was a sour sort of person, actually. Not that he deserved this. He got divorced a few years ago."

"That would have to be a pretty angry ex-wife."

"Are you making a sexist joke?" Ravenna said, looking hard at him.

"No, I didn't mean anything by it. Listen, our department is very strict about that sort of thing—"

"Don't worry."

Dorn said, "He was living with a wolf."

"What?" asked the policeman.

"From that new pilot project. He had a female wolf in his house."

"Well, that's useful information. I'm not even sure if we have a record of who's got what. It makes perfect sense, now that you mention it. The nature of the tearing, the extreme violation of the muscles, the drag marks on the ground. I'll let the team know not to just barge into his apartment, in case the wolf has returned. They might get an unwanted welcome. Of course, it might have headed into the forest."

"What will they do with the wolf, assuming they can catch it?" Dorn asked.

"Good question. If it were a domestic animal there'd be no debate—they'd put it down. But a wolf? This is more a question for the lawyers. Speaking of them, didn't you go to law school, Dorn?"

"Architecture. But I never finished."

"All the better, as far as I'm concerned. Listen, you two better move along. Before you go, Dorn, is there anything else you know about this Leev that might be useful?"

"He liked to drink coffee," Dorn said.

Little Bells

The traditional time for funerals in the village was Thursday morning. No religious reason or historical precedent was known that might explain why; that was the conclusion of a long and mind-numbing article in the village's historical news-letter, a publication with just over a hundred subscribers (including Dorn). The time was only one of several peculiarities surrounding burials here, but born-and-bred villagers like Dorn were so used to them that funerals attended elsewhere were the ones that seemed off.

There were three cemeteries, but over the years they had crept closer to one another so that soon, for all intents and purposes, there would be only one. They were on a long, gentle rise that sloped down again to the river, and a much-repeated joke had it that the residents of the old age home could eat their supper while gazing upon their next address. Dorn spent the first hours of that Thursday working on the scheme for the burning house. He always made a precise and accurate plan (his few months in architecture had proved to be of some use after all) before cutting any wood. Normally he would show the plan to the customer for approval, but in this case he didn't know who the customer was and so decided on the rare pleasure of satisfying himself.

At breakfast Dorn had turned to the newspaper, expecting to find a story about Leev. Surely death by wolf was sensational enough to take the front page away from the village council meeting and reports on this year's fishing season. But there was nothing on the front page, the second, or the third. It was on the second-last page, below a supermarket ad, that Dorn finally found it.

Villager Did Not Seek Help

Fifty-two-year-old Leev, born in the village and long-term resident of Linder Row, was found dead near the river on Wednesday. It was known that Leev had been suffering from depression since the end of his marriage, and the coroner has made a preliminary finding of suicide. It is common knowledge that the village has fewer than half the suicides of the national average, and the police do not expect that statistic to change much this year. It is believed that the deceased did not seek help from mental health professionals.

Leev was an employee of the village brewery, a position he'd held since leaving school. He was also one of the first residents to participate in the Wild Home Project. It is possible that the animal in his care, a female wolf, may have tried to assist him. Authorities are currently trying to locate the animal.

"Assist him?" Dorn said out loud. "Suicide?" If that wolf had tried to assist Leev, Dorn thought, it must have read his miserable mind and helped put an end to him. He couldn't tell whether this was an example of the local paper's typically incompetent reporting or if the police, and perhaps the village council, were trying to hide what really happened. Perhaps they feared lawsuits or political fallout. Well, Dorn was no private detective; it was more useful for him to wash the dishes than speculate on such matters.

At ten thirty he hung up his apron, changed his shirt, and brushed his beard. Deciding against appearing on his tricycle, he gave himself enough time to walk in the morning sun. As he arrived at the wooden cemetery gate, he could hear the tinkling of the small bells that hung on the trees between the graves. An article in the historical newsletter had suggested that the original purpose of the bells was to scare away birds and other animals from the nearby forest that liked to search in the freshly disturbed earth of a new grave, but in Dorn's mind the ethereal sound had become indelibly associated with death. He knew that Leev had belonged to a small religious sect and his wife had converted for his sake. He hadn't seemed to practise since his divorce, but Dorn supposed he hadn't renounced it either, and sure enough there was the minister in his black-and-gold robe, gathering a small group of mourners around the grave.

As Dorn approached, he saw several people he knew: other residents of Linder Row, a couple of lower-management employees of the brewery, the young woman who had given Dorn the bag of coffee at the Happy Café, and all three players in Leev's weekly game of Virsht. He had hoped to see Ravenna but now remembered that she hadn't actually known Leev.

Dorn joined the circle around the coffin. Apparently, he had missed the first prayers, for the minister was starting to speak. "We are here," the minister intoned, holding a handful of the traditional crushed snail shells in his hand, "to mark the passing of Leev from this world into the next. It is a journey that all of us, no matter how craftily we dodge and weave, must one day take. But who was this Leev who now exists in our collective memory? He was not a man at ease—with himself or the world. Not a man content or comfortable with the life that had been given to him or that he had made for himself. He struggled. He chafed. He looked life bitterly in the eye and spat. Is there not something impressive in this defiance? Even if it was a mistake, if it wasn't the right way, it was still courageous. And he shared those struggles with us—"

A noise came from the other side of the circle, half sob, half cackle. Dorn looked over and saw Leev's ex-wife, Jurma. She wore a long black dress with black stockings, a hat, and dark sunglasses.

"As I say," continued the minister, "Leev shared those struggles with us who knew him. He faced his own personal darkness and tried mightily to overcome it. He broke from the chains that held him, and he ran for freedom. Perhaps he ran into the eye of God Himself. Please let us join our voices together."

The minister began to sing, and the mourners joined in as he sprinkled the crushed shells onto the coffin while it descended into the ground. Now the mourners turned to shake hands or embrace one another.

Dorn had begun to walk away when he heard his name called. Turning, he saw Jurma taking off her sunglasses as she approached him. He'd assumed she was hiding her cynicism with those glasses and didn't expect to see her eyes so ravaged from crying.

Now she attempted a smile. "Hello, Dorn. It's been a while."

"I can't say I ever thought to see you back in the village, Jurma. You were so glad to escape it."

"I never thought I'd be back either. And when I heard, I had no intention of coming. But then I found myself buying a train ticket, and here I am. I'm surprised Leev considered himself still in the faith. I left it years ago, myself. All that empty rhetoric. Eye of God, my ass."

This was the straight-talking Jurma he remembered. "I suppose he has to say *something*."

"Why not say that Leev made an insane decision to take a carnivorous animal into his house and that the wolf showed her appreciation in the only way she knew how? By eating him."

"She didn't actually eat him."

Jurma shrugged. "And how are you, Dorn? Still making models?"

"I don't really know how to do anything else."

"Found yourself a lady friend?"

It was only now that Dorn remembered what was perhaps a suppressed memory: that one holiday eve, when Jurma and Leev still held parties in their house, she had made a drunken, unhappy pass at Dorn in the bedroom where he'd gone to retrieve his coat. After he had gently pushed her away, she'd looked at him unsteadily and said, "Why did you bother to put on a coat when you live next door?" Then she had let herself fall, laughing, onto the bed.

Now Dorn said, "Ah well, you know me."

She looked at him and something in her face changed. She started to take in short, panicky breaths. "It's . . . it's hard," she gasped. "You fall in love with someone and he gets into your blood. You stay and stay because, despite your supposed independence, you are afraid to live without him, you won't be able to survive. And then finally you get up the strength to break away. You make a whole new life, a much better life, but you find that in some way you were right—you never can really live without him and you've been ruined, completely ruined, unable ever to…"

She leaned forward, her eyes rolled upward, and she fainted. Fortunately Dorn, whose reflexes were usually glacially slow, put out his arms to catch her. Two women he didn't know hustled over to take her from him. Dorn quietly made his getaway.

⚜ 13 ⚛

Baart and Sons

Unlikely as it seemed, a new occupant moved into the house only five days after Leev's death. The police took down the yellow tape that had been strung around the property, a truck pulled up with a disposal bin on the back, and a gang of men carted out the entire contents of the house. That same afternoon a second crew arrived to clean and paint the interior. A moving truck appeared the following morning.

Although he was curious about the new resident on the street, Dorn was not the "Hello, neighbour, I've baked you a plosk" sort. He preferred to run into the person casually. He did catch sight of a harassed-looking woman trying to control three school-age children; there wasn't any sign of a partner, male or female.

Every day Dorn went to the Happy Café as usual, and when a customer entered he always looked up, hoping to see Ravenna. Until he remembered that it was the dreaded parent-teacher interview season, as she called it, when Ravenna would be too busy. As a result he managed to read more of *Vordram*, a long, philosophical passage in which the Wood-cutter compares his axe to a human—the iron head to a skull, the carved wooden handle to the curving spine—and wonders whether an object can desire love, both spiritual and carnal, and whether it is better to be a human or an axe.

After his fourth day in a row of reading on his own, Dorn walked back to Linder Row and stopped to watch another truck pulling up to Leev's old house. On the side of the truck were three lines of old-fashioned lettering:

BAART & SONS
Wildlife for Domestic Happiness
Government Certified

The new neighbour stepped out onto the front porch, pulling her housecoat around her. She motioned, unnecessarily Dorn thought, for the truck to back up onto the sidewalk. When the rear of the truck was only a metre or so from the porch steps, the engine sputtered off.

Two men got out and came around. The woman propped open the door, allowing the children to spring out, but she shooed them back inside. The men signalled to one another and then simultaneously opened the rear doors. One of them dashed forward, yanked down the corrugated ramp, the end of which hit the ground with a clang, and leapt away again. Both the men backed off. Dorn watched, fascinated, yet nothing seemed to happen. And then a large animal—yes, it was a bear!—lumbered down the ramp, moving its head from side to side the way a blind person might while listening to music. The bear paused at the bottom, then turned and made a low, guttural sound at one of the men, who stepped backwards and fell onto his ass. The bear padded on, fur rippling from the muscles beneath its shoulders, up the porch steps (the woman must have retreated inside, but Dorn hadn't noticed), and into the house, its fur mashing against both sides of the door frame.

The other man ran to shut the door of the house. The two pushed in the ramp, slammed the rear doors, scrambled into the truck, and backed up so quickly that they rode up onto the opposite lawn, leaving tire marks in the grass as they pulled away.

Dorn felt his own heart pounding. He went into his house and drank a tall glass of water at the kitchen sink. First a wolf and now a bear, and what was it doing at this moment? Tearing open the sofa, galumphing up the stairs after the children?

And yet it wasn't his business, so he went back to work on his commission. The four sides of the house had been made from thin sheets of high-quality birch plywood. He had drawn the windows and now proceeded to cut them out, starting with drill holes and then using a coping saw and files. He finished the base and ran a thin bead of carpenter's glue along the edges of the sides and placed them carefully, using straps and clamps—a tricky business—to apply pressure while keeping everything at right angles. It needed to dry overnight, so he switched to working on the external architectural details, lintels and ornaments that were to be cut from poplar blocks or half pieces of dowelling and then carved by hand using his sharpened gouges.

By the time he put down his tools and stretched out his cramping fingers, the sun was down. He took off his apron, trying not to trail wood chips and sawdust as he went to take a shower. Too tired to cook, he picked up the telephone to order a pizza.

"It's going to take an hour," said the voice on the other end.

"Are you serious? It's usually less than thirty minutes."

"I know, but a lot more people are staying in. Might be this animal thing. People not wanting to leave a wild creature alone. At least, that's what the boss thinks."

"Yes, all right, thanks."

Dorn popped open a can of Forgel beer, mass-produced stuff he preferred to the local ale, and turned on the television. For an hour he surfed channels: a twelve-year-old girl who sang like an old bluesman, a game show that had people dressing up as clowns and throwing pies at one another. He settled on an old black-and-white ski romance, and when the pizza came, he put the box beside him on the sofa. A patter on the windows alerted him to the start of rain, which was soon pelting the house like stones. He watched and ate and before long reached into the box only to find it empty. Pushing it aside, he lay down on the sofa, dozing off and then rousing himself only to close his eyes again.

The doorbell sounded. Most of the houses on Linder Row had brass knockers, but the tenant before Dorn had installed an electronic chime. Dorn looked at his watch and saw that it was almost 1:00 a.m. People rarely came to his door, and certainly not at this hour. He remembered his father telling him how, in his own childhood, peddlers were constantly coming to the house to sell jars of spelnberry jam or mats woven from the rubber of old car tires. Nowadays there was no place for such marginal people.

Dorn got up, brushing off pizza crumbs. He yawned all the way down the hall and opened the door.

And saw Ravenna.

She was soaked from the rain, her hair plastered down, her cheeks flushed and glistening, the outline of her nipples visible beneath her shirt.

"Is everything okay? What's happened?"

Ravenna looked into his eyes and then leaned forward and pressed her damp lips to his. "Dorn," she sighed. "Dorn, Dorn, Dorn."

And then he woke up. Still on the sofa, still with pizza crumbs on his shirt. He put the box in the recycling bin and went to bed.

❧ **14** ❧

Bail

For the next week, Dorn did little but work on the burning house. The vivid dream about Ravenna gave him an urgent need to get out of his own head, and the only way he knew how was through his hands.

The mysterious commissioner had given him licence to do as he pleased. He had decided that all the windows would be dark or curtained except for three, one per floor.

On the first floor an old man would be sitting in an undershirt and boxer shorts at his kitchen table. He would be playing the solitary card game Ramet while drinking a glass of ale. On the second floor the window would show a bathroom. He imagined old plumbing, with a raised enamel tub and tile walls. A child would be in the tub, its face and shoulders visible above the bubbles, one hand holding a toy boat.

The third-floor attic window—that would be the room on fire.

He had never worked so many hours or with such concentration. By the end of each day his eyes stung from looking through his magnifier. His back ached from hunching over. Each night he fell asleep instantly, not to wake again until daylight and without any lingering dreams.

One morning, opening the front door to fetch the newspaper, he glanced up at a house across the way and saw a row of small faces staring at him through an upstairs window. The faces bobbed up and down, got pushed aside, and appeared again. He was pretty sure they were otters. He remembered that his neighbour had a small pool taking up his whole back garden, the kind with a powerful current that allowed a person to swim continuously while remaining in place. He could only imagine what the otters made of that.

Even while working harder, Dorn kept up his habit of going to the Happy Café. Ravenna still didn't show. He found it difficult to read *Vordram*, especially as he had entered that long section, known colloquially as "the abyss from which no student returns," in which the Woodcutter falls into an unfathomably deep hole. As he falls, the reader is given a series of darkness similes that continues for almost two thousand lines.

Needing a break, Dorn picked up a discarded newspaper and found an article he had missed in the morning.

Wild Home Animal Project—Success or Failure?

There is no longer doubt that the people of our community have embraced with genuine enthusiasm the idea of living alongside wild animals. Conservative estimates put the number of registered homes at thirty-five percent, and while some of those have not yet received an animal due to the high demand, most are already living with one and sometimes a flock, gaggle, or swarm.

"We believe it's because of the children," says the village mayor, Lorkiin. "We did not count on the influence they would have on their parents. Kids these days are engaged and knowledgeable. They know all about climate change, pesticide damage, and poaching. Our children hold the key to the future of this planet."

Lorkiin admits that "inevitable" problems have arisen. Some animals have naturally proven more popular than others. There is, for example, a waiting list for snowy owls, while at the same time the program has yet to find a home for a velveteen tarantula after it was removed from a family that proved to be keeping the creature in a glass terrarium in violation of the program's explicit regulations.

At the same time, Lorkiin dismisses the recent surge in emergency room visits, up twenty-three percent over last year. "There are many possible causes that could be unrelated to the program. And has even a single participant complained? No. Besides," Lorkiin says with a chuckle, "our interns can use the practice with needle and thread."

At the end of the week, Dorn was ready to work on the third-floor window, which he had kept accessible by leaving off the roof. He would create a student's room, with books shelved haphazardly (including a miniature copy of the purple-covered *Vordram*), a desk with a goose-neck lamp, a row of black-and-white snapshots on the papered wall. The curtains pushed to either side of the window would be in flames, as would the door behind. The figure, a female in a nightgown, would be leaning out the open window, one hand on the windowsill and the other waving for help. At three and a half centimetres high, the figure would not be identifiable, but still Dorn was careful not to give it the features of anyone he knew. That is to say, he was careful not to make it look like Ravenna, in case he might—consciously or not—create a scene in which he could imagine heroically rescuing her.

When the figure was done, he dabbed a spot of glue on the bottom of the feet (carved and painted, although they wouldn't be seen) and placed it carefully. He was holding it still, looking at his watch as the glue dried, when the telephone rang. He waited another thirty seconds, gently let go, and went to pick up the receiver.

"Dorn, I'm so glad I got you."

"Ravenna?" His heart leapt. "What's wrong?"

She gave an embarrassed laugh. "I need rescuing, I'm afraid. Would you mind coming down to the police station?"

"You're not hurt?"

"No, no, nothing like that. And if, well, you could bring your chequebook."

Was he dreaming again? No, not this time. He did as she requested, putting his chequebook into the inner pocket of his jacket and then phoning the village's only cab company, Glipp Brothers. It was run by twins who had become less alike as they grew older, one slovenly and the other neat, their habits reflected in the condition of their cabs so that people hoped to get Glipp One rather than Glipp Two. But when he called, Dorn got the answering machine, which meant that both were out. They were notoriously slow to arrive even when free, and so there was nothing for him to do but drag his delivery tricycle out from the back.

It was late afternoon and the sun was over the opposite roofs. Riding the trike when in a hurry was always an unpleasant experience, and within minutes he felt knives shooting up his calves. Dorn pressed on, not even slowing when he saw three enormous birds clustered around something on the sidewalk. The birds were vultures, with hooked beaks and naked necks, and one turned its head to watch him as he passed while the other two pulled at the insides of whatever they were eating. It appeared to be a small orange cat, possibly the one that liked to shit in Dorn's own backyard.

He reached the station, his legs screaming with pain. The building was a modest wooden affair with painted gables, like a winter lodge. Dorn got off his bike, gave his aching lungs a moment to recover, and went up the steps. Inside, it was just as pleasant, at least up to the oak counter, behind which was visible a modern police station with computer screens, file cabinets, and bulletin boards covered in mug shots. Approaching the counter, Dorn saw his old classmate Boolnap at a computer, his police cap laid beside the keyboard.

"Excuse me, Officer Boolnap."

"What's that?" the policeman said, looking up. "Oh, it's you again, Dorn." He sounded less friendly than at their last encounter. "This is peculiar, isn't it? We don't see each other for decades, and now twice. I'd almost think it wasn't a coincidence."

"Certainly it's a coincidence," said Dorn hastily. Like most people, he didn't feel comfortable speaking to a policeman, as if he were guilty of something he couldn't quite remember.

"Let me guess why you're here. It's got something to do with the woman we brought in"—he squinted at the screen— "Ravenna. You were with her when we met along the river."

"That's right."

"And you also knew the victim, Leev."

"Well, it really is a small place, this village."

"Yes and no, Dorn, yes and no. But in any case, I suppose you are here to pay Ravenna's bail."

"I am," Dorn said, wondering what on earth she might have been charged with. He took his chequebook out, and Boolnap spoke to the secretary, who presented the proper paperwork. The secretary said that a certified cheque was required.

"I'll vouch for his being good for it," Boolnap said. "But I hope I won't have to keep stretching my neck out for you, Dorn."

"Thank you," Dorn said, deciding not to mention that this was the first time. The amount was enough to give Dorn pause, but he filled out the cheque, handed it over, received a receipt, then sat on a bench to wait.

❧ 15 ❧

Crime

Dorn waited forty-five minutes before Ravenna came through an unmarked door, accompanied by a female officer. He nodded at Ravenna, but neither of them spoke until they were outside. Then Ravenna draped her long arms around Dorn's neck and sobbed. It was some time before she managed to get any words out.

"I'm humiliated. And I'm so sorry to drag you down here."

"Don't think twice about it. Why don't we get away from here?"

The two looked at Dorn's delivery tricycle. "I forgot that I came here on this," he said. "Not a very glamorous getaway vehicle."

Ravenna laughed between tears. "I'm certainly not going in the basket. We'll just have to ride double," she said.

So Dorn got on and she pressed onto the seat behind him. He began to move down the street. He was tired from the furious ride to get there, and now with the added weight of Ravenna he could only move at a very moderate speed. The advantage was ease of talking.

"You don't have to tell me anything if you don't want to," he said chivalrously, although in truth he did feel entitled to know something.

"All right," she said. "I'll tell you. Even if it is embarrassing—"

Ravenna stopped speaking, for at that moment an animal crossed the road in front of them. Low and narrow of face, bushy-tailed, and carrying something in its teeth. Dorn could see that the animal was a fox, more rust than red so that the white underside stood out less. The fox stopped to adjust the bundle that dangled from its jaws.

"Oh my God, that's a baby!" Ravenna cried, one hand moving to her mouth. "It's holding a baby by the diaper. We have to do something, Dorn!"

"No," Dorn said. "It isn't a baby. It's a doll. A very realistic doll, do you see?"

The fox trotted on. Ravenna said, "You're right, thank goodness. Did I ever get a fright! But why is the animal in the street?"

"I don't know," Dorn said. "Perhaps it hasn't read the village council's rules. Listen, my legs are killing me. Can we stop for a bit?"

They were beside the park, the same one where Dorn had seen Ravenna practising with her hoop. So they got off the trike and sat on a bench. A couple of older kids were huddled near a climber at the other end, but otherwise it was deserted.

"All right," Ravenna said, looking into the middle distance. "I'll spill the beans. It's about your brother."

"Vin?"

"I found out that he was cheating on me."

"Cheating?"

"I know! Can you believe that? It's so vile."

"I mean, you were having a relationship with my brother?"

"That just shows you how self-destructive I can be. Vin! I don't even like him. He's nothing like you. But still, there's something that drew me to him. And of course it was all hot and steamy at first."

"I'd really prefer not to—"

"And it was such a relief to be with someone who hadn't lived his whole life in this damn village. Who had, you know, a larger view of the world."

"I did leave for a few months," Dorn said disconsolately.

"Even if it wasn't a view I agreed with. At all! In fact, I was thinking of ending it and then—bang." She slapped her knee. "The reality hits. It's so sordid. I found another woman's undies under the bed. He didn't even hesitate to confess. He practically bragged about her."

"The bank teller," Dorn sighed.

"Who?"

"She was getting dressed when I visited last."

"She wasn't a bank teller! She was a law student visiting her parents. So there's *another*?" Now she smacked her forehead with her palm, almost a comic gesture. "Doesn't that just figure. And really, it serves me right."

"But I still don't understand," Dorn said. "Why were you arrested?"

"Oh, right. Something you don't know about me is that I can have quite a temper."

"Anyone would have been angry. Did you throw something?"

"Not exactly. I grabbed a pair of scissors, jumped on top of him—he was still asleep in bed, the rat—and cut off his hair. That's right, I cut off that luxurious Samson hair of his, at least as much as I could before he woke up. And you know what? Part of it was a weave! He's going bald in the middle. Ha!"

"So giving someone a haircut against his will qualifies as a crime?"

"Assault, as it turns out. But only if the asshole turns you in. Vin phoned the cops right after I let him up. I didn't run away either. I stood there and gave him a piece of my mind until that stupid Officer Boolnap showed up. And the whole time, Vin was looking in the mirror and weeping. Actually weeping, if you can believe it. He cares more about his hair than me, that's for sure."

They sat in silence for several minutes. Dorn tried to take in all that he'd heard. He couldn't remember a more disagreeable feeling than he had now, knowing that Ravenna had been intimate with his brother. Of course, she was a free person and, unlike Dorn, actually acted on her emotions. And then he remembered that his brother knew about his feelings for Ravenna. Couldn't Vin have just left her alone? Perhaps he had done it as one more act of rivalry, the way he had needed to prove himself superior since they were kids.

"I am going to pay you back," Ravenna said. "I can cash a bond. Of course, I don't plan to skip bail, so I'll get it back in time. Do you think they'll make me do jail time?"

"I can't see that," Dorn said. "This *is* your first offence, isn't it?"

"Now you think I'm a career criminal! Yes, it's my first."

"Then no, I'm sure they won't. The thing you have to worry most about is your job."

"Holy bells, I didn't think of that. My job. What if they fire me? Or worse, take away my teacher's licence so I can't even go to another school? I love teaching. It's all I ever wanted to do besides throwing that stupid javelin. Not teaching would ruin my life. Listen, you've really been my white knight. I can't thank you enough. Now I think I better spend some time on my own. I'll walk the rest of the way home. I need to think this over and figure out what to do."

"Of course, Ravenna. Whatever's best."

"One more thing. Would you please, please come and speak to my class? That would be a real feather in my cap. It might help persuade them that I'm indispensable."

"I really don't think that my appearance—"

"But would you?"

"Anything you wish."

"Come this Friday. That's our day for special events."

She smiled unhappily, squeezed his hand, and sprang off the bench to walk quickly away.

✄ 16 ✄

Gun

Dorn did not go home. He waited until Ravenna was gone from view and then he got on his bike and began to pedal towards the river.

It felt as if he had learned more about Ravenna in the last half-hour than he had in all the months of their having coffee together. Of course, she wasn't some old-fashioned girl, waiting for Dorn to get up the courage to fall on one knee and declare his adoration of her. All this time she had been behaving like a normal, healthy person, having adventures, experiencing emotional highs and lows, letting herself get carried away and then regretting it. Yes, he would have preferred that his short, powerful, hairy-legged brother had been left out of the equation, but Dorn had to acknowledge that it wasn't his choice and in fact had nothing to do with him. He checked to see if his own feelings, now layered with more complications, had changed. But they hadn't. She was still Ravenna and he still adored her. He would have to tell her that, and sooner rather than later.

But first things first. He got to the river path, the pains in his legs reduced to a dull throb, and rode along until he reached his brother's glass mausoleum of a building. While he really wanted to tell his brother what he thought about using people so callously, he would hold himself back. Instead, he would ask Vin to get the police to drop the charges against Ravenna. That was what mattered.

Once again, the doorman showed no sign of recognition as Dorn wrote in the guest ledger. He took the gliding elevator up to the penthouse, but as soon as he stepped out he heard a startling noise behind his brother's door. It sounded like something breaking.

Dorn knocked. "Vin? Are you in there? Everything all right?"

"Is that you, Dorn? Thank the devil! Hurry! There's a spare key under the mat."

The fear in his brother's voice alarmed Dorn. Vin was still his blood after all, the younger boy Dorn had adored growing up. He found the key, opened the door, and went gingerly into the living room. Vin was standing on one of the white leather chairs. That his locks had been crudely cut off was nothing compared to the rest of his condition. He held his dangling left arm with his other hand. The sleeve of his shirt had been torn off and Dorn could see blood. There were more rips in his expensive trousers. But what frightened Dorn the most was the look on his brother's face.

"What's going on, Vin?"

His question was answered when he came around the sofa and saw the mink. It was crouched just before the chair, its luxurious fur puffed out, its fulsome tail swishing back and forth. The animal's pointed teeth were bared, and as Dorn came around, it turned its triangular head and hissed at him.

Dorn took a step back. "Why is it acting this way?"

"How the fuck do I know? It's a wild animal. And it's trying to kill me."

"Did you try to hurt it somehow?"

"Just go and get my gun, will you? It's in the drawer by the bed."

"You have a gun? Is it legal?"

"You want to debate the law right now?"

At that moment, the mink sprang up and bit Vin on the thigh before landing back on its feet. Several dots appeared on Vin's skin and then welled with blood.

"Ahh! Shit, shit, shit! That really hurts. He might have got an artery or something. Move it, Dorn! Get the gun!"

Dorn strode quickly along the outside of the living room, keeping an eye on the animal, until he got to the kitchen and passed through to the bedroom. Seeing the enormous bed with the high double mattress and tangled silk sheets, he couldn't help but remember that Ravenna had been in it. He opened the drawer and reached behind the tubes of gel and open packs of condoms to find the gun. It was not the enormous .44 Magnum he imagined from the movies, but a small pistol with a blue grip.

He picked it up, careful to point it down but away from his own shoes, and returned to the living room, where the animal was making a low growl in its throat.

"Go ahead," Vin said. "Kill it."

"I've never shot a gun. I might hit you by accident."

"Move to the left. Jesus, Dorn, think a little faster for once."

"Are you *allowed* to kill it? Technically, the animal belongs to the government, doesn't it? Maybe I should call—"

"Mother of Christ, Dorn, I'm going to shoot *you* when I get hold of that gun. Tell you what, I'll trade you for a confession. I was always jealous of you. You were the lovable one, and Mom cared more for you. The dumb one is always more loved. Is that enough? Go ahead and blast the thing."

Dorn looked at the gun. "That you were jealous of me is hardly a revelation." He took off the safety. "Here's what I want, Vin. I want you to make sure the police drop the charges."

"Charges?"

"Against Ravenna."

The mink jumped up towards Vin's face, higher than Dorn could have imagined possible. His brother screamed, and as the animal landed on its feet again, Dorn saw a flap of skin hanging from Vin's cheek.

"Ahh! God, that fucking hurts. I think I'm going to throw up. You're talking about Ravenna? What do I care about that skinny freak? Sure, I'll get them to drop the charges. Now shoot it, shoot it, shoot it..."

Dorn held out the gun, pointing it at the animal. He'd never killed anything in his life before—he even put terp bugs out of the house. But he put his finger to the trigger and pressed, and as the gun went off, he instinctively shut his eyes. The kick felt like someone giving him a shove, but it was immediately followed by an immense crashing sound. As he opened his eyes, the shattered glass was still falling from the window.

"You hit the fucking window! Do you know how much that glass costs? Damn it, Dorn, you couldn't hit an elephant. Shoot again and aim this time."

But there was no chance even to raise the gun, for the mink, no doubt smelling the outdoors, turned and leapt, neatly exiting by the open space without coming near the edges of remaining glass.

"Good riddance," Vin said, collapsing into the chair. "I hope it breaks its neck. Now get me to the hospital. You can drive me in my car. Just don't destroy that, too."

Dorn put the gun down on the end table. He picked up the cellphone from the table and put it into his brother's lap. "You forget that I don't drive. Call for an ambulance. And then phone the police station and get the charges dropped."

His brother looked up at him. The pain from the tear in his cheek was making his eyes water. Yet he somehow managed a ghastly grin. "This is quite a new side of you, brother. A shame that it won't last."

⊰ 17 ⊱

School Visit

It was a jubilant Ravenna herself who phoned Dorn to tell him she was no longer a wanted criminal. "I don't know what you did to convince your brother, but it worked. The school didn't even find out. Boy, do I owe you, Dorn. Anything you want, it's yours."

"Hmm," Dorn pretended to muse, holding a small saw in his hand. He couldn't recall Ravenna ever phoning him, although he had given his number to her a long time ago— just in case, he had said, she had any reason to get in touch with him. "I'm going to have to think about what I want."

"But just so you know, this doesn't get you out of coming to my class tomorrow."

"I would have assumed that you don't need me anymore."

"Are you kidding? I've told my principal, and he was thrilled. I scored some points, getting the great model maker into my class. Come at ten, will you? I can't wait."

Dorn had never given a presentation about his work. He put down the saw, removed his apron, and began to plan. He didn't fool himself into thinking it was primarily the kids he cared about, but at the same time he couldn't help wanting to hold their interest and perhaps even, if only in a small way, inspire them. Not to become model makers of course, but to look for an adult occupation that matched their genuine interests and talents. Working at something one enjoyed, he would show them, might be a better career choice than an occupation that brought in a higher income.

He didn't trust himself to speak off the cuff and so spent two hours laboriously writing out a script and then committing it to memory. He chose a selection of hand tools and a square of basswood to demonstrate on. Finally, he went to his computer and typed up a page with the title "How to Become a Junior Wood Carver." On it he made a list of inexpensive tools along with sandpaper and other items, as well as a simple pattern for making a key fob in the shape of a fish.

Coming back from the copy shop, Dorn heard the phone ring. He was right in guessing that Ravenna was on the other end. "Say, how about staying afterwards for lunch?" she said. "I'll pick up something for both of us and you can eat with me in the lounge and meet the principal and some of the teachers. I'll feel like a big shot."

"I'd like that," Dorn managed to say, his throat already closing with anxiety. Some of those teachers were Ravenna's good friends, which meant he would be on display for them. Making a good—or bad—impression could have a considerable impact on her view of him. After he hung up, Dorn went over his speech twice more, packed everything into his rucksack, and tried to watch television while eating some pickled smillings on toast. He went to bed, and must have actually slept a few minutes, although it didn't feel that way in the morning. He stood under the underpressured shower, then shaved and got dressed. He was too nervous to eat, so he had three cups of coffee, going over his speech again while checking his watch every five minutes until it was time to leave.

He arrived at the school during recess, the yard filled with screaming children. They raced, skipped, dug, pushed, laughed, blubbered, and generally acted as if they were absolutely mad. When the bell rang they streamed through the doors, leaving the yard strewn with candy wrappers, makeshift swords, even a discarded shoe. Dorn waited until the last child was well inside before following, although once the door was closed he had to press a red button and look into the lens of a video camera before hearing the lock click. This was his first time inside the school since graduation, but the smell was unmistakable, a combination of sawdust, damp clothes, urine, and disinfectant. The office, however, had been completely remodelled. The old high counter with a grille behind which the dour secretary had kept guard was now replaced by an island workstation where several children were assisting the secretaries.

A very small girl approached Dorn and politely asked what she could do for him. He told her his purpose, and she went to an electronic board, pushed a button, and said into a microphone, "The special visitor for Grade 3 is here!" Dorn expected Ravenna to fetch him, but instead two children, even smaller than the first girl, came up wearing homemade badges with the word *Ambassador* on them.

"Are you Dorn the model maker?"

"Yes, I am."

"Very good! Come with us, please."

So Dorn walked down the hall, a child at either side. The one on the right took his hand. Of course, he knew that Ravenna taught third form, but in his mind they had been several years older. He may have somewhat overestimated his audience. They walked down the hall, turned, and went up the stairs to the second floor. Ravenna's door turned out to be the one decorated with construction-paper flowers. Another clue would have been the din coming from inside.

The child let go of his hand while the other opened the door. The noise swelled and then ceased as the children stared. Seeing so many young faces turned his way was a disconcerting experience. He saw unruly hair, half-tucked shirts, juice stains, dirty mouths. One child, whose glasses had been fixed with electrical tape, gave him a mesmeric stare.

"Well, class, look who's here! Our special guest, Dorn the model maker."

Only when he heard her voice was Dorn able to take his eyes away and look over at Ravenna. She was standing by the board with a piece of chalk in her hand. There was a streak of white on her chin, but perhaps the children were used to that since they didn't pay it any attention.

"Please, come to the front, Dorn," she said. "The children are just so excited to hear you speak. We were looking at photographs of your models this morning. Of course, we've all seen them in the village shops. We took a vote on our favourites and, can you believe it, there was a four-way tie! Why, Bitel here"—she gestured to the girl in the glasses—"got quite upset because she couldn't decide *which* one she liked best."

"And Kohool voted twice," said the girl. "It wasn't fair."

"Now, now, I'm sorry I even mentioned it. I want everyone on their best behaviour, sitting still and with their listening ears on. Dorn, I hand the floor over to you."

He shuffled to the centre, in front of Ravenna's desk, while she skipped down to the back of the class and sat in an empty, child-sized chair. Dorn unslung his rucksack, ran his hands through his hair, and cleared his throat. "It's very nice to be here, children," he recited. "As you know, I have a rather peculiar profession. I am not a doctor, a lawyer, a plumber, or a house painter. In more wistful moments I look back upon my life and wonder how it is that I became the village model maker. Perhaps everyone wonders at some point how fate or accident or divine intervention has taken them on a certain path. My own path, although modest, is certainly an interesting one. But I must tell you that it is not something that happened magically or even easily. Instead, it took dedication, patience, and many years to develop the skills—"

At that moment a boy at the end of the first row turned his head and vomited. For such a small boy, he had held an impressive quantity.

"Oh dear, Voj, I thought you were looking green around the gills. Please, Bitel, take him to the nurse."

"I don't like him," said Bitel.

"Blagu, you take him. One moment, Dorn. I keep a bucket and mop in the corner. You'd be surprised how often this happens. I'll have it cleaned up in two shakes. Meanwhile, please continue."

Dorn watched Ravenna fetch the mop. Even after she cleaned up, the classroom retained a sour odour. He looked at the children, who stared at him with blank faces, and tried to remember where he had stopped.

"I have a suggestion," Ravenna perked up from the back. "When we were talking about your visit, the children had so many questions. Perhaps you would be so good as to answer some of them."

"Yes, certainly. That's a good idea."

Urgent hands went up. Some children were actually making small grunt-like noises. Not quite sure how to proceed, Dorn simply pointed to a boy in the second row.

"Did you ever make a lady with big breasts so you could touch them?"

"Dirkis!" said Ravenna sharply. "I don't know where that came from, but it's quite inappropriate. Perhaps Izzel has a proper question."

A girl in the middle stood up, although she didn't bother to remove the finger in her nose. "I like your models."

"Thank you very much."

"But my dad thinks they're stupid. Why do you make stupid models?"

"Well, I'm not sure…"

As he fumbled for a reply, a boy on the other side began to stomp his feet on the ground. "Did you ever make a whole army of little soldiers and then step on them with your boots? Because that's what I would do. *Stomp, stomp.*"

"I don't like him," the girl named Bitel said, pointing at Dorn. She started to cry.

"I'm a *Tyrannosaurus rex!*" said a boy, who began roaring and clawing at the one who was stomping his feet.

Ravenna scolded her students, but her voice was drowned out by the rising volume. Three children began to run around the perimeter of the classroom like circus dogs. Was there some way for Dorn to rescue the situation and earn the admiration and gratitude of the teacher? Perhaps by demonstrating. He opened his rucksack and reached in to take out the leather sleeve of tools. It was then that he noticed the little yellow river moving from under a desk towards him.

✥ **18** ✥

Patron

The instructions for delivering the model of the burning house came in an envelope pushed through Dorn's mail slot during the night. It gave an address, a room number, and a time.

Dorn had been pondering how to depict the fire itself. He considered breaking his own rule against any electric gim-crackery and putting in a flickering bulb. But in the end he decided against it. Instead, he drew rather elegant flames on a blank of highly streaked rosewood and cut them out carefully, spending considerable time filing and sanding the curling edges. He fitted them around the door and under the curtains, and if the effect was less immediately dramatic, its impact would, he hoped, be deeper.

After that he made the final touches, using a thin brush for the grout between the bricks and other details. As he worked he tried not to think about what he might encounter on delivering the model and who his patron might be, but of course it was impossible not to speculate. If this were a movie, Dorn thought, it would be someone known and yet unexpected, perhaps even hinted at in some earlier scene, at least in terms of motivation. The person who first came to mind was his brother. Dorn could imagine Vin making some big show of helping him out financially while actually trying to belittle him. But Vin wasn't even around, since after being treated for his mink bites he had flown to some tropical island to recover. After all, he assured Dorn before leaving, these days a businessman could make a fortune from anywhere in the world, as long as he had an internet connection.

Finally the model was done. Once again Dorn ordered a pizza and opened a beer. He didn't turn on the television but decided to catch up with *Vordram*, having missed some visits to the café after the classroom debacle, when he preferred not to run into Ravenna for a while. He sat on the sofa, took a bite, and read—

Did Woodcutter know the Animals had not been Formed
For his Pleasure and Use? Yeah is Struth. Yet Man-is-All
Or Swaggering thinks, as if his Bod would ne'er be Wormed…

Before long Dorn fell asleep, only to wake in the morning with a slice of pizza plastered to his shirt. He took a shower, then boxed up the burning house. He put on a light jacket and carried the box to his delivery tricycle after checking that the address was in his pocket.

Because Dorn had lived in the village his entire life, other than those two miserable college terms, he knew his way around too well to bother with addresses. Which was why he did not recognize the location of 7 Spallnoor, and it was only as he pedalled down it, towards the river, that he noticed that the only building after Lavinia Green was the back end of the old age home. And then it occurred to him that, although the home faced the Green, its designated address must be on Spallnoor.

"Huh," he said out loud, growing suspicious. Could the secret patron be his father after all? But as he walked around to the front door, lugging the protective box, he remembered that the address included a different room number. He found it on the first floor—second door after the dining hall.

Dorn knocked. He heard a voice and jiggled the knob with his two free fingers, just managing to get the door open. The room was identical to his father's in its dimensions and layout only, for the resident—who sat on the edge of the bed, pulling on a sock—had turned it into a shrine to the profession of firefighting. A row of helmets hung above the bed and an actual fire hose with its enormous nozzle dangled from the ceiling like a giant anaconda. The other walls displayed historical banners from various firehouses and vintage photographs of fire trucks spraying buildings. Dorn stood there, the box in his arms, taking it all in.

"When you've got arthritis, socks and shoes are tricky," said the man on the end of the bed. "Why don't you put that load on the floor." He had a rasping voice and, although not as old as Dorn's father, looked in worse shape. He was nearly obese, for one thing, and he had a noticeable tremor in his hands.

"It looks like I've come to the right place," Dorn said.

The man chuckled. "Indeed you have. I'm looking forward to seeing your handiwork. The rest of your money is in the envelope on the table."

"I think you should see the model first," Dorn said. "But may I ask your name?"

"What do you mean?"

"And why you keep it a secret from me?"

"I didn't put my name on the order?" The man made a circling motion near his ear with a finger. "No reason at all. Just forgetful these days. Why, if my head weren't screwed on, I'd lose that. My name is Plass."

Sometimes, Dorn thought, the answer to a mystery is that there is no real mystery at all. He took out his retractable knife and cut the tape on the top of the box, removed the packing material, and reached down to grab the base before lifting the model up and onto the small table.

"If you don't mind turning on the standing lamp, I'll see it better."

Dorn thought that the man, Plass, might get up to examine the model more closely, but he stayed on the bed, perhaps unable to move easily.

"Ah, it's good. Very good. Really quite beautiful. I like the way the architecture is so typical of the village. And that you haven't created some wild conflagration. That's a fire we might get control of. My hunch that it would be better not to give too many directions to an artist has been proven right. I see that it's a woman you've put in the window."

"Didn't you ask for a woman?" Even as he said the words, Dorn saw the letter in his mind. "Figure" was all the man had written. He said, "If you don't mind, may I ask why you want it?"

"A simple answer. Being a firefighter was not just my career of thirty-seven years. It was my love, my devotion. I never had a partner or children. I only had the firehouse and the fellows in it. They are all retired, too, or gone. It doesn't leave you with much, being too devoted to your work. But at least now I can look at your model and imagine pulling up in the old engine, hauling out the hoses, cranking up the ladder to the window. It'll be an aid to daydreaming, that's what it'll be."

Dorn chatted with the man for a while longer, until the old fellow began to tire. He picked up the money and they shook hands, after which Dorn left, closing the door behind him. He stood there a moment, feeling less deflated than usual, knowing that the man would enjoy what he'd made. The hall smelled of ammonia. From somewhere farther down came the sound of groaning—not an agonizing sound, more a constant complaint. While he was here, Dorn thought, he might as well visit his father, and so he went back to the lobby and took the winding staircase up.

❧ 19 ❧

Mountain

He was several doors away from his father's room on the second floor when he saw a pile of suitcases at the door. They were the old sort, with metal corners and leather straps and even some faded cruise-line stickers—the kind of luggage nobody used anymore except in store displays or to convert into coffee tables. While the meaning of their presence eluded Dorn, he became anxious enough to pick up his pace.

The door was open. He stepped in to see his father sunken into the armchair. A walking stick in his hands, he was dressed as if for an outdoor expedition, in flannel cap and jacket, forest-green pants with zippered pockets, and hiking boots. The closet door closed, making Torpe visible. She was identically dressed and carrying a large rucksack in one hand and a small one in the other.

"You ought to be able to manage this, at least, eh, Feenis? We'll put your pillow in it."

"What's going on?" Dorn asked.

"Look, you old scout, here's your son to wish you bon voyage."

"Did you pack my pudding?" asked Dorn's father.

"You saw me do it."

"Ah, but you're sly. You might have taken it out again."

"Why? So I could listen to you complain the whole way up the mountain? No, thank you."

"Mountain?" said Dorn. "You're not planning to climb Winzzel Mountain?"

"Do you know of another around here?" said his father. "When I was a young man I used to scurry up that hill without a care in the world. Used to take me three days to get to the top when everyone else took four."

"But you were twenty-three, not eighty-three. I don't understand. Why is your room all packed away? Torpe, what's going on?"

"I'll tell you what's going on," she said. "We're tired of this life, aren't we, Feenis? Staring out of windows. Watching hours of television. Living among a bunch of nincompoops. Eating nothing but pudding."

"I like pudding," said his father.

"Yes, we've established that," Torpe said. "I know what you're thinking, son-in-law, but this wasn't my idea."

"'Son-in-law'? You got married?"

"It's all Feenis. He wants a last adventure, a chance to smell the fresh air and slide on a glacier. Isn't that what you said, Feenis?"

"When I was twenty-three," Feenis said, "we unbuttoned our trousers and had sex right there on the moss. And she cried out and the gulls cried, too. Later we discovered the impression of a brachiopod fossil on her butt cheek."

"Well, you're not doing that with me, you old goat. Look at your son's face. He's gone pale. Don't worry, we've got professional mountaineers to assist us all the way. Strapping men. They've even got a chair to carry your father when he's tired. Seven days up and then we'll take the cable car down the other side. And after that we're not coming back to this tomb, are we, Feenis? We're off on a cruise."

"I'm going to use up all my money," Feenis said with a grin.

"If you don't like living here anymore," Dorn said, "you can move in with me."

"That dull life of yours would be worse than here," his father said. "No, I'm off. And if I die, they can let my bones bleach in the sun."

Dorn was about to protest again when he hesitated. Perhaps the two of them were right. Wasn't it better to have some last fun? Who was Dorn to tell another person what to do? Besides, he was relieved that his father didn't want to live with him.

"Just be careful," he said finally.

His father rose creakily out of his chair. He mimed climbing—referring to Winzzel Mountain, no doubt—taking one agonizing step after another, using his walking stick for balance. Then he mimed reaching the top, taking off his cap and putting it on the end of the stick to raise like a flag. "I'm on top of the world!"

"You old Beelzebub," said Torpe, smiling fondly at him.

Riding home again, it was difficult for Dorn to avoid reflecting on his own life. True, he had never wanted excitement and thrills, but he had yearned for pleasure and for love. If he hadn't suffered much in his life, he hadn't known real happiness either. And he certainly hadn't taken any risks, not even the risk of rejection. He had often covered for his own cowardice by telling himself that his friendship with Ravenna was so much better than nothing. But the reality—

Dorn stopped.

The bear.

Large, hump-shouldered, slathering at the mouth as it lumbered down the street after three kids on bikes. The kids looked both terrified and excited as they glanced back over their shoulders. The smallest, a girl, caught sight of Dorn and waved as she went by.

The bear ran after them, its back paws propelling it forward, front paws slapping the ground in near unison. He could hear the *huff-huff* of its heavy breathing until it turned the corner after the bikes and disappeared from view.

Dorn felt himself shaking. It did not stop until after he reached home.

❦ 20 ❧

Traits

For the first time in more than a year, Dorn did not have a new commission to work on. He took a second cup of coffee and proceeded to read the rest of the newspaper, including the scores of the local sports teams. After that he cleaned up his workspace, sharpening his tools while listening to some of his oldest jazz records. After lunch came laundry. It was during dusting and vacuuming that he noticed Vin's marquetry box on the bookcase.

He picked up the box and felt its weight. Not empty, but hardly heavy either. Shaking it gently, he felt something move back and forth. Then he put it in the centre of the kitchen table and sat down to contemplate it. Had his brother told him not to open it? Not exactly, at least as far as he could remember. Don't bother with it, he'd said. Now Vin, well on his way to healing, was no doubt picking up women in some tropical paradise even as their father was on his way to climb Winzzel Mountain. The only ones left in the village were Dorn and the remains of his mother.

He regretted not having thought to visit her grave after Leev's funeral; her section had been a two-minute walk away. His memories of her had grown increasingly faint, given that she had died when he was six, while on the other hand what he'd heard about her had frozen into an unchanging portrait. She had been the opposite of his father, a gentle and loving parent, and with a natural creative streak that had her arranging flowers on the dinner table, painting the door frames with patterns of leaves, turning little cardboard boxes into boats and airplanes for his delight. Who knows how Dorn and Vin would have turned out if she had been there to raise them?

He stared again at the marquetry box. Whatever was inside it, he didn't want to know. He got up, picked up his copy of *Vordram*, and headed for the Happy Café.

It had been a beautiful spring, beginning earlier than usual, and today there was a genuine feeling of summer in the air. The ground had dried out and the loamy scent was gone, while a second wave of flowers bloomed in gardens. Dorn took off his jacket and carried it as he walked past the shops and into the café. Upon entering, he looked to the table where Ravenna usually sat, but it was unoccupied.

"Hello, Dorn, the usual?"

"Yes, thanks. You haven't seen Ravenna, by any chance?"

"You missed her by about ten minutes."

He'd expected as much. His visit to her class still made his face burn when he thought of it, and he hoped a few more days might ease his discomfort. Their regular table happened to be the only one free, the others having been taken over by a group of tourists. They were sorting through postcards and various trinkets picked up in the shops. One man, who had clearly visited Tul and Tule's, held up a red lollipop in the shape of a woman's clitoris and was pretending to lick it.

Dorn took a sip of coffee, then looked at his book. He was a little worried about the lack of work and wondered if there was anything he could do about it. He had never advertised or approached potential customers and, besides, as far as he was aware, there were no new businesses in town. He could approach the small handful that didn't have models, but feared he'd get an icy reception; anyway, he rather admired them for *not* wanting one. Vin had often said he should come up with some cute carvings that could be reproduced on a mass scale by cheaply paid Third World workers. "Their work is excellent these days," Vin had said. "I bet the average person wouldn't be able to tell the difference between them and your original." But even if the idea was feasible, which he doubted, it wasn't his ambition to flood the world with more junk than was already cluttering it up.

These worries made it hard to concentrate, so he merely opened the bent and stained cover of *Vordram* to read the various student comments scribbled on the title page.

Reading this is torture
Good for ass-wipe
Suck my dick, Woodcutter
Who the fuck cares about this ancient garbage?

He looked up when a voice addressed him. "Would you mind if I shared your table? It's crowded today."

"No, of course," Dorn said, closing the book and looking up at the person, a rather old woman with long white hair, as she lowered herself into the chair. Dorn didn't generally notice clothes, but she wore a notably fine wool blazer, black flecked with grey. She put her own espresso cup on the table alongside a folder of neatly stacked papers. Dorn considered it rude to stare, a rule that so many young people seemed to dismiss, yet a suspicion made him glance several times at the woman's face—her clear blue eyes, almost invisible white eyebrows, leathery skin that came from spending time outdoors over many years. Yes, it was the author Horla. Now she noticed, looked up, and, understanding that she had been recognized, nodded.

Dorn cleared his throat. "Excuse me, but may I say that I found your children's book to be very interesting."

She smiled a little. "Very interesting, you think? A careful choice of words. Perhaps you mean it isn't good."

"No, no, not at all."

"Well, I'm not sure what 'good' even means anymore. I think a lot of people become more convinced of their long-held opinions as they get older, but I become less sure of mine. To be honest, I didn't want to publish it."

"No?"

She shrugged. "But I needed the money."

Dorn found it shocking that a writer like Horla, someone he thought of as an artist of high integrity, should take money into account. But of course she had to live, like everyone else.

The author looked at him and said, "May I ask what your role is in our village?"

"Model maker."

"Really? So you're the one?"

"Yes, that's me."

"I'm very glad to meet you. I have thought a certain amount about you. Or at least about the you I have imagined."

"Me?"

"Yes. The model maker. It has often seemed to me that you are the only person in this village with whom I share any common traits. Have you yourself never thought that?"

"I wouldn't have presumed to compare myself to an internationally famous author."

She made the disapproving *toosk-voosk* sound characteristic of the villagers. She said, "We both spend our lives making things. Things based on real life. We make them smaller and more manageable, so that they become quite harmless. We are both miniaturists, you and I. The only difference is that you present what is already visible and make it pretty. I prefer to show what is behind the walls or under the floor. Not so pretty." She chortled and took a sip of her tea.

Dorn wasn't sure if he should be flattered or insulted. He said, "But what if one did both? What if one showed what was pretty and then went behind the walls?"

"Ah!" she said brightly. "Then you get nominated for all the awards!" Horla laughed, throwing her head back and exposing her gaunt and rivuleted neck.

Dorn waited a moment before speaking. "If I might ask your opinion. You are a thinking person. Observant. Penetrating. What do you, a writer, make of this wild animal project, people bringing these creatures into their homes?"

Horla brought her cup to her thin lips and drained it. She said, "I believe it says just about everything about this town. It's all there, in a nutshell. Like one of your miniatures."

Dorn said, "From what I can see, it isn't a good thing for either the people or the animals. But what I can't figure out is the real reason behind it. Is it malicious? Or is it just a misguided idea that some people find romantic?"

She raised a pale eyebrow and then, picking up her papers, rose from the chair. "Well, I don't know any better than you, model maker. But I have learned that sometimes there is evil and sometimes there is stupidity, and not infrequently the two are so close as to be impossible to tell apart. It is an honour to have met you."

She nodded and picked up her staff, which had been leaning against the wall. Dorn watched her leave the café.

Seeing such a person, who lived as she chose rather than to satisfy others or just out of random accident, stirred Dorn. It made him feel as if he ought to find in himself the resolution to pursue what he truly wanted. He picked up the author's small cup and was tempted to slip it into his pocket as a souvenir but instead he grabbed his own as well and put them both in the dirty-dish bin.

❧ 21 ❧

Chase

Was it meeting Horla? Or the disturbing incidents with the animals? Or just becoming fed up with his own cowardice? Whatever the reason, Dorn decided to seize the moment. He would go immediately to the school, find Ravenna, and declare his feelings—no, not his mere feelings, but his love—to her.

He walked down the main street and then turned up, going past the park as he followed the route that he took home whenever he wanted to pass by the school in the hope— pathetic, it seemed to him now—of getting a glimpse of Ravenna in the window of her classroom.

"It's no longer enough," Dorn said aloud, stamping his foot self-consciously but still with a small feeling of triumph. Why, it felt good to be so determined, and he stamped his foot again. But this time when he did so he noticed that something in the park moved its head, attracted by his motion. Near the swings. At first he thought it was a dog, sniffing around in the hope of finding something edible that had fallen out of a child's pocket.

But the dog, staring at him now and keeping perfectly still, didn't look quite right. Its fur was too yellow, its flank too skinny, and its upright ears too narrow and pointed. It looked to Dorn like some kind of wild dog, a coyote or jackal or even a dingo. Not something he'd ever seen living around here. The mangy creature kept its eyes on him.

"Go on, scat!" Dorn said with more authority than he felt. Still, the animal didn't move. Instead, a second one appeared from behind the teeter-totter. It was smaller but with a more pointed jaw and teeth visible along the gums. Dorn tried to imagine telling Ravenna about it in a joking way, not quite confessing how unnerved he had been. And while he was thinking this, a third appeared near the sandbox, this one shaggier and much larger. Dorn thought that it looked more like a wolf, possibly even the same one that had belonged to Leev. Didn't that animal also have a streak on each side of its jaw? The animal stared at him with a kind of expressionless intensity.

Time for Dorn to make an undignified exit. He took a step forward. So did the dogs. He took two more steps and they followed. Another step, and the first one began trotting towards him in an almost casual way. The other two followed, the small one lowering its head and flattening its ears, and the one that looked like Leev's wolf hanging back a little. Dorn began to walk more quickly, but they, too, picked up the pace, and now the animals were beginning to close the space between them. The first one emitted a low growl.

It wasn't just unease Dorn felt now but flat-out fear. That there was no way he could outpace these wild creatures wasn't going to stop him from trying. He stumbled, caught himself, and started to run. Looking over his shoulder, he saw all three bound forward. They would have been on him in seconds if it weren't for the cast-iron fence that enclosed the park to keep children from running into the street. Dorn ran down the sidewalk, looking again to see them searching the inside of the fence. The wolf found it first and gave out a yip. All three burst through the open gate.

Dorn cried out, not words but some inarticulate sound. He pumped his arms and legs and leapt onto the road. He didn't see the car moving towards him until it swerved, and Dorn, sure he would be hit, found himself somersaulting on the pavement, his head banging on the cement. There came the screech of brakes, the sound of a heavy thump, breaking glass.

He lay there, on his back.

The car door opened.

"Holy fuck!" said a voice somewhere near him. "Is that you, Dorn?"

Dorn blinked and looked up and saw, upside down, the face of his former classmate Officer Boolnap.

"Aarrh," Dorn moaned.

"I think I killed it," the police officer said. "Whatever it is, I killed it."

"Where...where did the others go?" Dorn managed to say, afraid they would reappear and tear him apart.

"Ran off in the other direction. You're a lucky man, Dorn. That thing was almost on you. I didn't actually hit it on purpose, I was trying to avoid you. Here," he said, offering a hand.

Dorn got up painfully. He could see the dead animal now, lying on its side with blood in its mouth. The first one that had spotted him.

"Oh shit," said Officer Boolnap. "I've got to go."

"What? Where?"

"Didn't you hear the bell? There's a fire."

"A fire?" Feeling groggy, Dorn rubbed the back of his head.

"At the elementary school."

"The school?"

"Why do you keep repeating me? Yes, the school. Yesterday some kid brought a wild rat that had been living in his house to his class, snuck it in his lunch box. But it got out. Apparently, the rat's been gnawing on the wiring."

"I need to come with you."

"Fine, but hurry up."

Taking a step towards the police car, Dorn discovered it wasn't only his head that had got banged up: his ankle throbbed painfully. Looking up, he saw a shadow by the side of a post box. The shadow moved and the long face of the wolf appeared. It stood there, looking at him.

"If you're getting in, move it," said Boolnap. Dorn hopped to the passenger side, pulled open the door, and levered himself into the seat. Boolnap put the car into gear and started to drive.

"Why do you want to come, anyway? Wait a minute. It's that criminal woman friend of yours, isn't it? She's a teacher at the school."

"She isn't a criminal," Dorn said, wincing. "My brother deserved worse."

❧ 22 ❧

Jump

Because crime in the village had always been of the most minor sort, the police force was small and modestly equipped. Cars were square six-cylinder boxes, and although Boolnap put on his siren and pressed on the gas, they chugged at an almost leisurely rate up the hill towards the school. Also, Boolnap came to a full stop at every cross street. Dorn found that he couldn't contain himself.

"Damn it, Boolnap, can't you get us there any faster?"

But Boolnap looked as if he didn't hear him. In fact, this time when he came to a stop, he didn't start up again. Dorn was about to urge him on when he felt a strange vibration coming up through the floor of the car. Boolnap must have felt it first. The vibration grew stronger until it felt like a furious beating of drums. And Dorn could hear something, too, a low pounding that was impossible for him to make sense of.

As Dorn and Boolnap stared out the windshield, a splendid reindeer with an impressive rack charged across the intersection, its hooves kicking up stones.

"What the...?"

And then came a herd of perhaps two dozen, pounding along the road, snorting through widened nostrils, backs glistening.

"Well, I never," Boolnap said. A cloud of raised dust remained in the air. Dorn himself was speechless. Realizing that the car had stalled, Boolnap turned the key again and pulled slowly through the intersection. He drove no faster, but Dorn didn't say anything.

One more turn, and Dorn could see black smoke rising into the air.

"That looks serious," he said.

"I hope they've put a call out to the nearby fire departments," Boolnap said. "Ours isn't exactly impressive, even when it does arrive."

Two more streets, another hill, and there was the school, with a crowd watching from the other side of the road. As they pulled up, Dorn saw a few stragglers coming through the front doors with their hands over their mouths, teachers and parents holding the hands of students. Boolnap pulled up onto the curb and they got out.

"Back up, everyone," Boolnap said in his best official voice. "You don't know what could happen with a fire. A spark might fall. There could even be an explosion."

The crowd moved back a step or two. It wasn't yet hopeless, but flames could be seen flickering in numerous windows.

Dorn called out, "Has anyone seen the third-form teacher, Ravenna?"

"I saw her come out carrying one of her students," said a nearby mother, pressing her child against herself. "Her face was covered in soot."

"Yes, but she went back inside," said a man.

Dorn asked again, but nobody else had any information. He could not help feeling that this was some ordained, fated moment and that, like the Woodcutter in *Vordram*, who had at last to face the monster, he was being called upon to prove himself. "Ravenna," he whispered. Then he took a breath, clenched his jaw, and began to cross towards the school.

Boolnap came up and grabbed his arm. "Just what exactly are you doing?"

"She must be in there. I know Ravenna. She'd search every nook and cranny to make sure no kids were left behind. She might be trapped in there, unable to get through the smoke or flames."

"You're not trained for this, Dorn. And neither am I. We have to wait for the firefighters."

"I've been waiting all my life. Not anymore."

"Did you really just say that?"

Dorn shook off his old classmate and kept going. He limped painfully on his twisted ankle and made it to the front doors, taking out a handkerchief to press against his mouth and nose. As soon as he pulled open the door, he felt the heat. Inside, ash hung suspended in the air. Chairs were overturned and papers scattered. From somewhere above, the bell rang on, echoing between the walls. He remembered which class-room belonged to Ravenna, but it was just as likely that she was elsewhere, so he decided to take a quick look into every room as he passed. He opened closets, offices. He had forgotten how low the urinals were in the boys' washroom. He called her name over and over. When he got to the end, he opened the heavy stairwell door to climb to the second floor.

Here the smoke was more dense; it seared his throat. The air was hotter, too. Moving more quickly, he opened the first door and saw the window blinds melting like objects in a sur-realist painting. He moved down the hall, from one side to another, calling out, blinking tears from his eyes, trying to breathe through the inadequate filter of his handkerchief. Finally he reached Ravenna's classroom. The handle of the door was hot and he had to wrap it with the handkerchief. He tried to prop the door open, but it swung closed behind him.

In here the smoke was less dense. The only flames were engulfing a solitary desk in the middle of the room, as if by spontaneous combustion. "Ravenna?" he called, lowering himself to check under the furniture. He opened the back cupboards, although Ravenna was too tall to fit in one. As he stood there, deciding what to do next, the chair beside him whomped into flame. He jumped sideways, crashing into a hanging skeleton made from cardboard tubes. Now the skeleton caught fire. He began choking. He needed air.

The rising smoke made it difficult to see. His head throbbing worse than ever, he put his hands out and made his way to the windowsill. Smoke was being sucked out the window. He leaned out, coughing and spitting, trying to clear his throat. The smoke pulsed away for a moment and, looking down, he could see the crowd below. From farther away came the wail of a fire truck.

And then he saw more smoke. In the village—rising from one, two, from five different buildings. It looked as if everything might go up. And he was going to die here, in his childhood school, the site of so much of his early unhappiness.

Calm down, Dorn, he told himself. He tried to breathe regularly even as he saw someone below begin to cross the street to the school side.

"Dorn?" the figure shouted. "Is that you, Dorn?"

He recognized Ravenna's upturned face. "Ravenna, you're safe!"

"What are you doing in there? You have to get out now!"

"I came to find you. I love you, Ravenna."

"What?"

"I said I love you!" he shouted hoarsely.

"Move it, Dorn!"

So she wanted him to get out and save himself. He had to get out now. Turning around, he saw that the door was on fire. There was no way he could even get close to it. He turned around again. "I'll have to jump."

"It must be ten metres! Wait for the fire truck."

"I can hardly breathe."

"Fine, be stubborn. I'll just have to catch you."

"Catch me? Are you serious?"

"Hey," she called to the crowd across the street. "Can anyone help?"

But nobody crossed over, not even Boolnap. Ravenna shouted up at him again. "It's okay, I've got strong arms."

"All right. But don't try to catch me. Maybe just break my fall a little."

"Jump!" Ravenna commanded.

Dorn pulled himself up onto the hot windowsill. Ravenna moved in closer, holding out her arms. He began to lower himself by his hands, trying to catch his heels on the brick. A cry made him turn his head and he saw an enormous bird of prey, some kind of eagle with a wingspan like a dining table, swoop down from a nearby steeple.

"Ravenna, look out!"

She turned and put up her hands to protect herself from the bird's claws, even as Dorn's fingers slipped and he began to fall.

Epilogue

The instant Dorn woke, he knew what day it was.

The one-year anniversary of the day the village burned to the ground.

His apartment was on the ninth floor; he got up and went to the window to look down. He could see figures crossing the courtyard, a line-up at the coffee stand, somebody cradling a bundled infant, a delivery person on an electric scooter. Straight across, in the window of the opposite apartment house, a man was shaving.

Dorn made an instant coffee, warmed a bun in the microwave, and, while eating, he continued reading a mystery novel by Odom. It had been a bestseller for months and was soon to appear as an eight-part television series, and a fellow at work had told him he couldn't put it down. It certainly was easy to read: after a day, he was already halfway through it.

Dorn opened the fridge and picked out a couple of sausages, a triangle of cheese, and an orange for his lunch bucket. He put on his heavy-soled shoes, locked the door behind him, and headed for the elevator. As he got to the corner, the 481 bus was just pulling up to the stop. He tapped his pass and, though the bus was already crowded, found a seat near the back. He rode it for half an hour to the last stop, on the outskirts of the city, neither reading nor listening to music but merely looking out at the passing streets.

The hydraulic door swooshed shut behind him. Dorn stood on a gravel road, facing a row of identical industrial buildings. His own place of employment had a blue sign: *Jurdstik Furniture Manufacturing*. Much of the work was automated but there were still some twenty-five humans overseeing the machinery and checking that the right number of bolts and fasteners went into each box of unassembled parts. Dorn was one of three employees with any woodworking experience. It was his job to do the buffing of the Jurdstik traditional rocking chair, after which he would apply a sticker: *Finished by a Real Carpenter*. His income was not only steady but a good twenty percent higher than when he had been a model maker, plus benefits and paid holidays.

When the lunch whistle blew, he went out with the rest to the picnic benches on the green strip next to the loading dock. They were not bad sorts, the others, and sometimes he contributed to discussions of recent politics or played a few hands of Virsht before the whistle called them back inside.

All of his models, including the ones in the museum, had been destroyed in the fire. While the last one he made, for the retired fireman, hadn't actually burned (the old age home had been spared), Plass had thrown his valuables out the window just in case, and the model had shattered. A decade and a half's work gone. Dorn hadn't found out for several days after his fall, having been knocked unconscious on hitting the pavement. He'd also broken a leg and fractured a wrist. A helicopter had transported him to the city hospital, where he'd remained for several days, and since the houses of Linder Row had all been destroyed, there had been no reason to return.

He learned from the newspapers that the fire had burned down about sixty percent of the village. It had burned its way up the main street, turning historic buildings into charred shells. That nobody died, the newspapers declared, was a miracle. But the village would never be the same. For one thing, an unknown but clearly significant number of residents were opting not to return. For another, a consortium of developers (including his brother, Vin) was already rebuilding along new lines, replacing the main street with two indoor "shopping hubs." The new structures were going to be glass and steel, with solar power and other environmentally progressive features. To bring in visitors, a state-of-the-art interactive science museum called the Living Forest would be built, perhaps ironic since the moratorium on "harvesting" the real forest was coming to an end and its renewal appeared to be in doubt. As for the Wild Home Project, very little was written other than to recognize it as a "noble, if quixotic, failure."

After leaving the hospital, Dorn lived in a hotel for a month before finding his apartment. He'd still had a cast on his leg on starting work, but the company was glad to get him, having searched fruitlessly for a qualified person. In all that time, Dorn did not see a single person from the village—not until he ran into one of the servers from the Happy Café. She now had a job in a chain pub and told him that on the first Wednesday of each month a group of ex-villagers met for a drink. Dorn himself had little enthusiasm for going until he ran out of ways to find Ravenna.

He knew that she hadn't gone to the city hospital but to a clinic at the nearby university, requiring stitches in her scalp. Also that she, too, did not return to the village. He woke up to find a card on his bed, a reproduction of a postcard from the previous century showing the village's former main street. *Get better soon! Love, Ravenna.* But there was no address, her old phone number didn't work, and after he learned how to navigate the various social media sites, he could still find no trace of her. And so he had started to go to the Wednesday-night pub meet-up for the sole purpose of hearing something about her. He encountered such people as his brother's former doorman, who had never spoken to him in the village and now greeted him like a long-lost friend. Tul and Tule, the former sex shop owners, turned out to be working as greeters in a discount superstore. He drank a Forgel beer while listening to others argue about whether the burning of their village was a catastrophe from which they would never recover or the best thing that had ever happened to them.

And then came last night. A man drank three shots in a row and began to enumerate the ways in which his wife (at first, Dorn had thought he'd said "life") had changed since they came to the city. Somewhere in his monologue of complaint he mentioned that his son was going to a school where the former village teacher Ravenna was now employed.

"Which school is that?" Dorn had asked, a tremor in his voice.

"Number 618, in Eyers district. And what's more, my wife is now cooking completely different meals for dinner, she's into all this foreign stuff…"

When the final whistle blew, Dorn cleaned himself up in the factory washroom and took the bus home again. He got off several stops early to do some errands. There was a large supermarket near his apartment, but he preferred a row of specialty shops—bakery, greengrocer, butcher, fishmonger— that he had to admit reminded him of the village, except that there was nothing particularly quaint about them.

Among them was a small book and gift shop, one in the Toska chain. Imitation cherrywood shelves, soft lighting, pop music playing from invisible speakers. Most of the shop was taken up with pens and journals, birthday cards, small puzzles, and the like, but the front window always had a few new books displayed. Dorn paused to look, as he enjoyed seeing the attractive covers. And here today was a new book by Horla. *Conflagration.* It had the size and look of all her books, a black cover with white type and a blurry black-and-white photo—in this case, what looked like a dollhouse in flames.

Strangely enough, he did not go in to buy it. On another day he might have, but right now Ravenna was too much on his mind. Besides, he was already late for his last stop—the veterinarian's. He crossed the road, walked to the end of the block, and went in.

There were two people sitting in the chairs—one with a cat in a carrier, the other with a parrot on her shoulder. "There you are," said the woman behind the desk. "I think your Fibsi is dying to get out of here."

She picked up the phone and spoke to someone in the back. A few minutes later, a young woman in blue scrubs came out with Leev's wolf on a leash. Not Leev's anymore, of course, but Dorn's. He'd named her after a cartoon dog from a television show he'd watched as a child.

"So she's all right?" Dorn asked.

"Yes, but you've got to be more careful. She'll eat another sock or maybe worse if you let her. Happens with former strays sometimes. They never get over the fear of starving."

"Well, thank you," he said, taking the leash. "Come on, Fibsi. Let's go home."

Dorn hefted the grocery bag onto his opposite shoulder, and they started down the street. At least the animal had learned not to pull on the leash. They trotted along the street together and turned the corner, where a small boy holding an ice cream cone stared at them.

"Is that a wolf?" the boy said.

"She looks a bit like one, doesn't she? But no. She's part husky and part torkl and a bit of shepherd."

"She looks scary, anyway."

"To be honest, she doesn't much like kids."

The boy backed away as they continued on. After the fire she'd been found and given a DNA test; it turned out she hadn't been wild but only mistreated and abandoned. It was his old schoolmate Boolnap who had telephoned in search of a new home for her, telling Dorn that not a single remaining village inhabitant would agree to take her in.

"She definitely didn't kill Leev, then?" Dorn had asked.

"Well, it isn't as if she were tried by a jury of her peers," Boolnap had replied. "Let's just say that charges were dropped for lack of evidence."

Feeling as if he didn't have all that much to lose, Dorn had agreed. Besides a few behavioural issues, the animal had proved to be good company, following Dorn around the apartment or lying next to him on the sofa with her head in his lap. They reached his apartment house, took the elevator up to the ninth floor, and stepped over the junk mail just inside the door. Dorn put the groceries away, then fed the dog. He poured himself a glass of water and picked up the mail to throw away. Tucked among the flyers was a postcard from his father.

Dorn—
    Fact: most countries have some form of pudding.
    When somebody says to you, "It's never too late," they are probably trying to put something over on you.
    We keep going, to the ends of the earth!

—Feenis

Dorn sat down at the kitchen table (the apartment had no dining room) and drank the glass of water. Fibsi came over to lie at his feet. Dorn looked at the marquetry box in the middle of the table, waiting for the day when it might seem right to open it. It had somehow survived the fire, with only its bottom blackened. The village council had sent it to him along with a couple of gouges, their handles burned away, and some unplayable vinyl records. Dorn picked up the box. After all, yesterday he had discovered the whereabouts of Ravenna. When ought he to open it if not now?

He judged the box to be about two hundred years old, going by the geometric inlay pattern. Back then, artisan workshops had lined the river near the village. There had been no distinction between what a person did and who he was, much like the Woodcutter in *Vordram*. Even as a model maker, Dorn had been a mere shadow of those long-dead makers.

It was, he knew, a secret box or lockbox, tricky to open due to a series of wooden slides; the top had to be shifted in one direction, the side in another, then the bottom, four or five times in the right order. In reality, any inquisitive snooper could get it open after ten minutes of trying. Dorn shifted it about until he was able to slip off the top.

Inside was a small, palm-sized carving of an animal. The workmanship was crude; it might have been a dog, cat, sheep, or something else. Of course, he recognized it as the first carving he had ever made, lying in bed as an ill teenager and using the cheap blades given to him by his uncle. Not long after he finished it, the carving had disappeared from his bed-side table. He'd searched frantically and been saddened by its loss, and for years afterwards he could poignantly recall that feeling. It had never occurred to him that his younger brother had stolen it.

Holding it now, he tried to read his own feelings. Vin had taken it, and now Vin was, in his usual twisted way, giving it back. So what *did* he feel? Something akin to how he felt on coming to the end of one of the mystery novels he'd taken up reading. The revelation was always a little disappointing, never matching the suspense that came before. Perhaps back in the village it would have meant more to him, but here, in this new existence, when he was no longer a model maker, it meant very little.

Dorn chopped up the vegetables and the meat he had bought and stir-fried them together in his new wok. He opened a Forgel beer, sat down at the white melamine table, and ate. He was sorry now not to have picked up the new Horla.

The Eyers district was a few kilometres away, but Dorn had a new bicycle—a used touring bike with twelve speeds. He washed up, put on his jacket, and went to the door. Fibsi came up and started to whine. "Do you really want to come?" Dorn said. "I suppose you could use a good run. Come along, then."

He snapped the leash onto Fibsi's collar, and they took the elevator down. There was a bike rack behind his apartment from which good bikes were regularly stolen, but so far the thieves hadn't considered his to be worth their while. Dorn had been used to the stately pace of his old tricycle, but here in the city, cyclists zoomed along the bike lanes at tremendous speeds, ringing their bells to make pedestrians leap out of the way. He looped the end of the leash on his wrist, and they started off, the dog easily keeping up. Unlike the streets of the village, much of the city was still unknown to him. He had to stop several times and consult the GPS coordinates on his cellphone until he finally reached City School Number 618. Locking up his bike, he looked the building over while Fibsi stood by his side. It was early evening, the sun already going down, teachers and students long having abandoned the school for the day. This wasn't anything like the old brick edifice of the village; instead, it was a single storey made of large and colourful blocks, with square windows and a futuristic cantilevered roof. So here was where Ravenna now taught her class. He knew there was nothing magical about his having found the address, for it was merely the result of dogged persistence. He wasn't even as sure of his feelings for Ravenna as he once had been. And even if he and Ravenna did manage somehow to get together, perhaps they would make each other miserable and last a few months or a year before breaking up. If that turned out to be the case, wouldn't it be better just to forget the whole thing and not, as he had planned, take an afternoon off work so as to be standing here when Ravenna came out? At least then the memory of their friendship would remain unsullied, although it was true that he wasn't even sure that he cared so much for those memories anymore.

Looking at the school, he thought of the last pages of *Vordram*, which he had finished after finding a copy in the hospital library. The Woodcutter's encounter with the monster had been surprisingly brief, a mere dozen lines or so in which he raised his axe to fell the creature. The whole poem had led up to this moment, only to let it go by in the most cursory fashion. And yet, unlike with the mystery novels, he hadn't felt the slightest disappointment. The Woodcutter had slain the monster at the exact moment the monster had killed him, sending the Woodcutter's head into the air. His body had fallen, and the small white flowers that were the nation's emblem had grown from it. The very last line told of the spot being forgotten "now and forever." How satisfying that forgetting was, that now and forever.

As Dorn stood beside his bike, thinking about the end of *Vordram*, one of the school doors opened. It opened and out came Ravenna.

A low growl from Fibsi. "Shush now," Dorn said under his breath. The animal quieted. Ravenna turned to lock the door behind her. But when she closed the door, the hem of her skirt became trapped. Shaking her head, she unlocked the door to release herself and closed it again. Then she put away the keys and straightened her clothes, and taking a step forward, looked up and saw Dorn.

She frowned. It might have meant anything, that frown— for example, that she couldn't quite tell who he was, since they were a bit far apart and she wasn't expecting him. He had a sudden desire to grab his bike and pedal away with Fibsi, but of course he had locked it to the post. And so he gave an awkward wave. She gave a tentative wave back. And they both stood there, looking at one another.

Acknowledgements

I have been a long-time admirer of Jay MillAr and Hazel Millar and I thank them warmly for bringing this work into the Book*hug fold. Peter Norman proved to be an enthusiastic and sensitive editor whose letters were themselves a model of good prose. I was glad to have Stuart Ross as the copy editor. My thanks to Samantha Haywood and her crew at the Transatlantic Agency. And finally to Rebecca Comay, Bernard Kelly, Sophie Fagan, and Yoyo Comay for reading the manuscript and giving me the nod.

AUTHOR PHOTO: JOSH LEVINE

CARY FAGAN is the author of eight previous novels and five books of short stories, including *The Student, Great Adventures for the Faint of Heart,* and *A Bird's Eye.* He has been nominated for the Scotiabank Giller Prize, the Writers' Trust Fiction Award, the Governor General's Literary Award for Fiction, and has won the Toronto Book Award and the Canadian Jewish Book Award for Fiction. He is also an acclaimed writer of books for children, having won the Marilyn Baillie Picture Book Award, the IODE Jean Throop Book Award, a Mr. Christie Silver Medal, the Joan Betty Stuchner—Oy Vey!—Funniest Children's Book Award, and the Vicky Metcalf Award for Literature for Young People. Fagan's work has been translated into French, Italian, German, Dutch, Spanish, Catalan, Turkish, Russian, Polish, Chinese, Korean and Persian. He still lives in his hometown of Toronto.

Colophon

Manufactured as the first edition of
The Animals
in the fall of 2022 by Book*hug Press

Edited for the press by Peter Norman
Copy edited by Stuart Ross
Proofread by Rachel Gerry
Type + Design by Ingrid Paulson

Cover image ©master1305/iStockPhoto

Printed in Canada

bookhugpress.ca